She should never have come back, Laura thought to herself.

The foolish dream she'd harbored for so long in that secret part of her heart—that for her and the children there would be a happy-ever-after—was just that, a foolish dream.

"I've been looking for you."

Laura gasped in surprise and glanced up to see Tanner standing in the doorway, staring down at her with eyes black with anger and something more— was it pain?

"Just when were you planning on telling me? Or were you planning on going back to the city without saying a word?"

"How..." she began, then broke off, realizing that what she had hoped to avoid had in fact happened. Bravely she met his penetrating gaze as the shock of learning he'd uncovered the truth quickly wore off, leaving in its wake a feeling of relief... relief that she no longer had to live in the shadow of her deception.

Dear Reader,

The holiday season is upon us and what better present to give or receive than a Silhouette Romance novel. And what a wonderful lineup we have in store for you!

Each month in 1992, we're proud to present our WRITTEN IN THE STARS series, which focuses on the hero and his astrological sign. Our December title draws the series to its heavenly conclusion when sexy Sagittarius Bruce Venables meets the woman destined to be his love in Lucy Gordon's *Heaven and Earth*.

This month also continues Stella Bagwell's HEARTLAND HOLIDAYS trilogy. Christmas bells turn to wedding bells for another Gallagher sibling. Join Nicholas and Allison as they find good reason to seek out the mistletoe.

To round out the month we have enchanting, heartwarming love stories from Carla Cassidy, Linda Varner and Moyra Tarling. And, as an extra special treat, we have a tale of passion from Helen R. Myers, with a dark, mysterious hero who will definitely take your breath away.

In the months to come, watch for Silhouette Romance stories by many more of your favorite authors, including Diana Palmer, Annette Broadrick, Elizabeth August and Marie Ferrarella.

The authors and editors at Silhouette Romance love to hear from our readers, and we'd love to hear from *you!*

Happy reading from all of us at Silhouette!

Anne Canadeo
Senior Editor

NO MISTAKING LOVE
Moyra Tarling

Silhouette
R O M A N C E™
Published by Silhouette Books New York
America's Publisher of Contemporary Romance

To my parents.
In loving memory.

SILHOUETTE BOOKS
300 E. 42nd St., New York, N.Y. 10017

NO MISTAKING LOVE

Copyright © 1992 by Moyra Tarling

ISBN: 0-373-08907-4

First Silhouette Books printing December 1992

All the characters in this book have no existence outside the imagination of the author and have no relation whatsoever to anyone bearing the same name or names. They are not even distantly inspired by any individual known or unknown to the author, and all incidents are pure invention.

®: Trademark used under license and registered in the United States Patent and Trademark Office and in other countries.

Printed in the U.S.A.

Books by Moyra Tarling

Silhouette Romance

A Tender Trail #541
A Kiss and a Promise #679
Just in Time for Christmas #763
All About Adam #782
No Mistaking Love #907

MOYRA TARLING

is the youngest of four children born and raised in Aberdeenshire, Scotland. It was there that she was first introduced to and became hooked on romance novels. After emigrating to Vancouver, Canada, Ms. Tarling met her future husband, Noel, at a party in Birch Bay—and promptly fell in love. They now have two children. Together they enjoy browsing through antique shops and auctions, looking for various items, from old gramophones to antique corkscrews and buttonhooks.

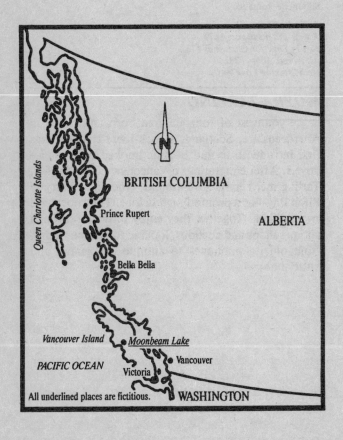

BRITISH COLUMBIA

ALBERTA

Queen Charlotte Islands

Prince Rupert

Bella Bella

Vancouver Island — *Moonbeam Lake*

PACIFIC OCEAN

Vancouver

Victoria

All underlined places are fictitious.

WASHINGTON

Chapter One

Laura Matthews glanced out of the kitchen window of the lodge to where her five-year-old twins, Carly and Craig, were helping Mac McLeod finish stacking the firewood he'd been chopping for the past hour.

Owner and operator of the summer resort, Mac took pride in doing everything he could to make a vacation more enjoyable for the folks who rented his cabins and campsites on the lake.

As she watched the threesome work together, she wondered, not for the first time since her arrival a month ago at the Moonbeam Lake Resort on the west coast of Vancouver Island, what Mac's reaction would be if she was to tell him that Carly and Craig were actually his grandchildren.

The answer was simple, He wouldn't believe her. And even if he did, she knew that telling him his son Tanner McLeod was the twins' father would be hard for Mac to swallow.

Neither Mac nor Laura had seen Tanner for six years—not since the funeral of Tanner's younger brother, Billy. In his grief and despair Mac had blamed Tanner for Billy's death, vowing neither to forgive nor forget.

Tanner wasn't responsible for his brother's death, of course. Billy had been alone in his car when he'd crashed into the concrete abutment near the railway tracks on the road leading to the island highway.

Laura felt her eyes fill with tears and she blinked rapidly as a cavalcade of memories of that unforgettable night suddenly threatened to overwhelm her.

"Mommy! Mommy!" The eager cries of the twins brought Laura out of her reverie and she quickly wiped away a stray tear before turning to face them.

"Hi! What's all the excitement about?" she asked as she reached for the towel on the hook nearby and began drying her hands.

"Mac's going fishing and he asked if we'd like to go," said Craig, who was usually the spokesperson for the twosome. Ten minutes older than his sister, he was much more outgoing than Carly.

"Can we?" Carly asked, and Laura crouched to her daughter's level and gazed into eyes the exact cornflower blue as her father's. Laura felt her heart skip a beat and wondered if Mac had noticed how much Carly looked like Tanner.

"*May* we," Laura corrected. "And yes, you may." She chuckled softly as the two of them exchanged delighted grins before turning and racing toward the door.

"Don't forget to put on your life jackets," she called after them, knowing full well Mac wouldn't let the twins near the jetty unless they were wearing them.

Laura absently tucked a strand of chocolate-brown hair behind her ear and returned to the sink where she'd been rinsing the lettuce for the evening meal's salad. Her plans to take the summer off and spend more time with the twins had quickly changed when she'd heard Mac was in need of a cook for the season. A chef by trade she'd had no problem persuading Mac to give her the job, though she'd sensed he was curious about her reasons for wanting to spend the summer at Moonbeam Lake. She smiled to herself as she saw Mac help the twins with the zippers of the life jackets before handing each of them a small fishing pole.

During the past month she'd watched Mac slowly get to know his grandchildren. That he enjoyed having them around was clear by the way his lined face lit up the moment they appeared each morning. And Laura marveled at the way he took such pains to answer the numerous questions Craig asked him and at how he'd smile encouragingly at Carly whenever she ventured a question of her own.

The children in turn adored Mac, and Laura suddenly found herself dealing with feelings of guilt brought on by the knowledge that not only had she been depriving the children of a grandfather, she'd been depriving Mac of the joy of knowing the twins and being a part of their lives.

But coming back to Moonbeam Lake hadn't been easy. Much as she loved the place, not all of her memories of it were happy.

With great deliberation Laura firmly closed the door on the past. Rehashing it would serve no purpose whatsoever. What mattered was the present and the future and deciding what was best for the children. But she was in the throes of a dilemma: should she try to find a way to tell Mac about Carly and Craig or should she continue to keep the secret she'd been living with for the past six years?

The fact that Craig has already begun to ask Laura questions about his father and what had happened to him added another dimension to her problem. So far, she'd managed to avoid giving her inquisitive son a direct answer, but she wasn't sure how long she could keep evading the issue.

She didn't want to lie to the children. But how could she tell the twins that their father was a highly acclaimed photographer who didn't even know he'd fathered a child, let alone twins—or that on the night the children were conceived he'd been so distraught with grief over the loss of his brother that he'd believed he was making love to another woman?

Tanner McLeod slowed the rented car he was driving and rolled the window down. He waited impatiently for a break in the oncoming traffic that would allow him to make the left turn off the main island highway on to the road that would take him home.

Home. The word slipped into his mind bringing with it an abundance of memories, some pleasant and others achingly painful.

After successfully completing the turn, he continued along the familiar route, comforted by the fact that other than a few new ruts here and there, no major changes had been made to the road.

He stepped on the brake, slowing the car to a crawl as he approached the railway crossing and abutment where his brother Billy had died.

Even after all this time, Tanner only had to close his eyes for a moment and the vivid image of Billy's car crushed against the concrete wall leaped instantly to mind.

Cursing under his breath, he forced himself to relax his grip on the wheel, but it was several minutes and a good five miles farther until he felt the tension within him slowly begin to ease.

It wasn't long before he reached the turnoff for Moonbeam Lake. Tanner felt his heart pick up speed as he made the final turn and headed toward the ridge overlooking the lake.

The moment the lake came into view, shimmering like a bed of diamonds in the afternoon sunshine, he was suddenly assailed with an array of conflicting emotions. The sharp sense of joy that washed over him was immediately followed by a piercing pain.

He couldn't look at the lake and not think of Billy and the times they'd fished together or gone swimming in the cool, clear waters or skinny-dipped on a hot summer's night.

Tanner pulled over to the side of the road and turned off the engine. He had to take several deep, steadying breaths before stepping out into the sunshine.

He let his gaze slowly take in the panoramic view, and as always he was stunned by the incredible beauty of the scene before him. He'd taken numerous photographs of the lake from every conceivable angle, but the photographs he carried everywhere with him were a far cry from the real thing.

A rush of memories crowded in as his eyes came to rest on the lodge built by his father more than forty years ago. Made from logs, the sprawling two-story cabin blended beautifully with its surroundings. The main floor consisted of a living room, kitchen and dining room, as well as a small games room, bathroom and porch. Four bedrooms filled the second floor and above them lay the attic. A feeling of contentment settled over him. He was home.

He should never have stayed away so long, he admonished himself silently as he drank in the sights and sounds and smells surrounding him. It was good to be back!

Until now he'd stayed away, allowing the demands of his job, coupled with his father's refusal to talk to him or to answer the letters he wrote, to influence him. And for a time he'd almost given up hope of ever reconciling with his father.

Six years ago Tanner had witnessed the devastating effect Billy's death had had on Mac. In his pain and grief he'd lashed out at Tanner with a bitterness that had driven a wedge between them and compounded Tanner's own feelings of guilt and regret.

But Mac had been too wrapped up in his despair to see that Tanner was grieving, too; instead of drawing them together, the tragedy had widened the rift between them until it became a chasm as deep as the Grand Canyon.

Friends kept telling Tanner his father needed time— time to come to terms with Billy's death, time to see reason, time to learn to forgive.

Well, his time was up. Tanner thought. Six years was long enough to be angry at anyone.

But making peace with his father wasn't the only reason Tanner had returned to Moonbeam Lake. At this thought his gaze shifted to the secluded stretch of sandy shore near the old flat rock that marked the end of his father's property.

Tanner had a ghost to lay to rest . . . the memory of a woman who six years ago had silently offered him comfort at a time when his world had been shattered into a thousand pieces; a woman whose scent still haunted him in his dreams; a woman whose gift of herself that traumatic night had eased his torment enough to make him want to go on living.

Not without some effort Tanner brought his thoughts back to the present, noticing the sun had disappeared behind a huge black cloud and that more storm clouds were steadily gathering over the ridge of mountains on the far side of the lake.

Summer storms weren't an unusual phenomenon in this part of the country and he knew, even before he felt the breeze begin to pick up and stir the grass and nearby tree branches, that sometime within the next fifteen minutes the storm would hit.

Laura stood on the patio and frowned at the darkening sky. Five minutes ago the sun had been shining brightly, but now there were only glimpses of blue sky between the threatening clouds and a breeze was tugging none too gently at the trees and stirring the usually calm surface of the lake.

As she made her way down the path toward the jetty, she noticed that most of the dozen or more boats Mac rented to the campers holidaying at the lakeside resort had returned. She noted with some relief that Mac and the twins were also heading to shore.

Behind her she heard the sound of a car's tires crunching to a halt on the gravel driveway in front of the lodge. She glanced quickly over her shoulder but she didn't recognize the car.

As far as she knew, no campers were expected to arrive today. But the resort wasn't full, in fact there were several cabins available for rent, as well as a number of campsites in the campground behind the main lodge. No doubt whoever it was had seen the sign for Moonbeam Lake Resort on the highway and had come to check it out.

The twins were calling and waving to her and Laura focused her attention on the boat as it drew near. Grabbing for the rope Mac threw her, she secured it to the jetty before pulling the small craft alongside.

Reaching over, she lifted Carly out and set her safely on the jetty. She turned to give Craig a hand but he was already scrambling out under his own steam.

"Need any help?"

At the sound of the deep familiar voice Laura felt her heart slam against her rib cage in startled response. Dear God! It couldn't be, a voice cried inside her head.

Her glance flew to Mac, taking in the look of stunned disbelief on his face. For a fleeting moment she saw a glint of emotion flicker in the depths of his blue eyes, before it was quickly suppressed.

"Tanner! What the devil are you doing here?" Mac asked tersely as he stepped from the swaying boat onto the jetty.

"*Who* are *you?*" Craig's question forced Laura to turn and look at Tanner.

She'd fantasized a million times about what she'd say and do should she ever meet Tanner McLeod again. But nothing had prepared her for this moment. Coming face-to-face with him after six long years, had as devastating an impact on her as being hit by a speeding train.

When her gaze locked with his, her mouth went dry and for a moment she thought she might faint. She fought the dizzying sensation with every breath, acknowledging in that secret corner of her mind that he hadn't changed . . . that he was still the most incredibly attractive man she'd ever met.

"Laura . . . I thought it was you," Tanner said, his mouth curling into a smile. "What a pleasant surprise."

Laura was saved from having to respond when the air was suddenly split by a resounding crack of thunder. Within seconds huge drops of rain began to fall from the sky, bouncing off the wooden jetty and splashing on the lake's surface, creating ever-increasing circles on the water.

Carly squealed in surprise and fright, and grateful for the distraction, Laura tore her eyes from Tanner and bent to scoop up her daughter.

"Come on. We'd better make a run for the house," she urged her son who'd been staring up at the stranger with undisguised interest.

"What about my fishing rod?" Craig queried, darting a worried glance at the boat bobbing on the choppy water.

"Go," Mac ordered. "I'll bring your rod," he added as he reached into the boat to retrieve the fishing gear.

"Hurry!" Laura urged as she began to move off the jetty.

"Give me your hand," Tanner said and at his words Craig threw his mother a questioning glance.

"It's all right," Laura quickly assured him. "That's Tanner, he's Mac's son."

Craig switched his gaze to Tanner and without further comment accepted his outstretched hand.

Another clap of thunder reverberated in the sky above them, and this time Carly let out a scream and buried her face against Laura's chest. Laura immediately broke into a run and headed for the house.

Less than a minute later, soaked to the skin, she reached the shelter of the porch. She was gasping for breath as she opened the screen door and stumbled inside.

Carly clung to Laura, shivering and wet, but Laura was relieved to note she wasn't crying. Moments later Craig and Tanner joined them.

"Wow! That was fun!" Craig announced, grinning up at Tanner.

"You said it," Tanner replied, returning the smile as he released the boy's hand to wipe the water from his own face.

Laura watched the brief exchange and felt a moment of panic. "Craig, sweetheart. Go to the laundry room and bring me some towels, please?" she asked, wanting to separate father and son, afraid Tanner might see the faint resemblance between himself and the boy smiling up at him.

"Okay," Craig said, and raced down the hall.

"They're twins, right?" Tanner questioned, smiling at Craig's departing figure.

"Right," Laura replied, sure he could hear the thunderous roar of her heart.

"Are you here on vacation?" he asked, turning to her.

Laura swallowed nervously. "No, I heard Mac needed a cook, so I hired on for the summer," she explained, wishing Craig would hurry back.

"Just like old times," Tanner said, but before Laura could respond, Mac appeared on the porch.

"Here's the towels, Mom," Craig said, returning from his errand, carrying two bath towels. Thrusting one at his mother, he offered the other to Tanner.

"Thanks, you're a pal," Tanner said.

Craig nodded and rushed to open the door for Mac. "Did you get everything from the boat?" he asked.

"Yes," Mac replied, drawing a ragged breath. "It's all out there on the porch," he added as he wiped his face with the sleeve of his shirt.

"Get a towel for Mac," Laura told her son as she set Carly on the floor and began to dry the child's face.

"Here, use this one." Tanner offered the towel to his father.

Mac gazed at his son for a long tense moment, no warmth or welcome in his expression. "I want nothing from you," he muttered, and ignoring the towel he strode past Tanner and disappeared down the hallway.

Tanner flinched as if he'd been struck, and seeing his reaction, Laura felt a pain stab her heart. Her eyes met his fleetingly and she saw a look of despair flash briefly in their depths.

"Still the same old stubborn..." Tanner muttered under his breath.

"Mom? What's wrong with Mac?" Craig asked, a puzzled frown on his face.

"Ah...I expect he just wants to get out of his wet clothes," Laura said as she gently towel-dried Carly's short, dark curls.

"But he sounded angry," Craig said. "Is he mad at me?" There was no mistaking the hint of anxiety in the boy's voice.

"No, son. He's not mad at you," Tanner was quick to assure Craig, but at his choice of words Laura threw a fearful glance in Tanner's direction.

Don't be ridiculous! she chided herself silently. Tanner couldn't know that Craig was his son. The only person who knew the truth about the twins was her mother, Irene.

"What's he mad about?" Craig persisted.

"He's mad at me," Tanner told him.

"Why's he mad at you?" Craig wanted to know.

"Craig, that's enough," Laura said firmly. "You're much too inquisitive for your own good. Let's go upstairs and find you dry clothes."

"Me, too, Mommy," Carly said, struggling to free herself from Laura's ministering hands.

"Do we have to?" Craig asked with a sigh.

"Yes," Laura insisted, as she stood up. "Supper is almost ready and I need the two of you to help me set the tables in the dining room," she added, knowing how the children loved to run around the spacious dining room, carrying the cutlery for her.

"Come on, Bro," Carly said, using her favorite nickname. "Race you." Without a backward glance she scampered off in the direction of the stairs.

"Cheater..." Craig called out as he raced after his sister.

The silence that followed their noisy departure was broken only by the sound of the rain pounding on the roof of the lodge.

"I'd better go and supervise," Laura said, noticing with some embarrassment that her wet T-shirt was clinging to her breasts in a rather provocative way. She felt her face grow hot and she lowered her eyes, hugging the towel to her chest.

"I bet there's rarely a dull moment with those two around," Tanner said with a smile, noticing as he spoke the blush that tinted her cheeks. The fact that she seemed both embarrassed and nervous puzzled him. She'd always been rather quiet and shy, but her reaction was more in keeping with that of an innocent young girl than a mature married woman with two children.

"You're right about that," Laura replied, holding on tightly to the towel. She started to follow the children, then came to a halt. "I'm sorry. I don't mean to abandon you. I guess you'd like to change out of your wet clothes, too."

"Yes," Tanner agreed. "But first I'll get my suitcases from the car."

"Oh dear...I forgot...the twins are in your room." Laura's tone was apologetic. "I can move them if you like," she added quickly.

"No, please, don't do that," Tanner said. "I'll take the spare room."

"Actually, I'm in the spare room," Laura said, beginning to feel a little foolish. "The only empty room is..." She hesitated and her eyes flew to meet Tanner's.

"Billy's," Tanner finished for her, and Laura saw a flash of pain in his eyes when he spoke his brother's name.

"Look, I can move the twins in with me...that was the original plan when we arrived. If you wait until after supper it won't take long to rearrange things." Laura knew she was rambling but she couldn't seem to stop.

Tanner smiled and shook his head. "No, don't disrupt them. That wouldn't be fair. It's really not a problem. Billy's room will be fine," he assured her.

"If you're sure..."

"Positive," he announced firmly, before turning toward the screen door and slipping outside.

As Laura made her way to the stairs, her thoughts lingered on Tanner. It was obvious that despite Mac's decidedly chilly reception, he intended to stay. But for how long?

When she'd made the decision to take on the job of cook-housekeeper at the resort for the summer, she'd done it for a number of reasons. She'd wanted the children to meet and get to know their grandfather—even if neither knew it—and she'd wanted them to experience the great outdoors; to appreciate the beauty of nature.

The summers she'd spent working at the resort had been some of the happiest times of her life and she wanted the children to create memories of their own.

While living in an apartment with her mother in downtown Vancouver had its advantages—mainly its proximity to the restaurant she and her mother owned and ran there—Laura often felt guilty that Carly and Craig didn't have a backyard. A good deal of their time was spent indoors with her mother or a sitter, and only occasionally did they get taken to a park to play.

"Has he left?"

The question brought Laura's musings to a halt and she glanced up to find Mac standing at the top of the stairs.

"No, Tanner hasn't left," Laura said as she reached the landing, and at her words she saw a look of surprise and relief flit across Mac's face.

"Oh..." Mac seemed slightly flustered by her answer. "Well I don't know what he thinks he'll accomplish by staying. I didn't invite him here, you know."

"Mac...he's your son. Surely he doesn't need an invitation," Laura said gently.

"He shouldn't have come." Mac said, before abruptly turning and making his way to the back stairs.

The sound of the children's voices growing ever louder drifted down the hall, and with a sigh Laura headed in the direction of Tanner's old room.

Above her she heard a rumble of thunder but this time it lacked its earlier fury. Perhaps the storm was already moving on, she thought absently.

Or was it? Tanner's unexpected arrival had created quite a stir, not unlike the storm, but somehow she doubted that he'd leave as quickly or as quietly.

Chapter Two

Tanner set his suitcase on the floor before softly closing the door to Billy's bedroom. Dropping his cameras on the foot of the bed, he crossed to the window to stare at the lake.

Outside it was still raining heavily and the black clouds hovering over the mountains looked like a war party regrouping for another attack.

The bedroom had originally been Tanner's, but the fall he'd left to "see the world and make his fortune," Billy had moved in and claimed it as his own. Billy had been eleven years old at the time and he'd hated the fact that Tanner, his big brother and best friend, was leaving.

Billy had been two and Tanner ten when their mother died from complications arising from a bout with pneumonia. Mac hadn't known how to deal with the loss of his wife, let alone how to comfort his sons, and as a means of working through his own pain, Tanner had taken over the care and feeding of his younger brother.

Though there was an eight-year gap in their ages, they'd shared a close relationship. A smile curled at the corner of Tanner's mouth as memories of Billy drifted into his mind—of the time when he was five and had tagged along with Tanner on a hike around the lake. They'd come across a small herd of deer grazing in a clearing, and Tanner had been amazed that Billy had managed to stay both still and silent while Tanner snapped a roll of film.

Tanner had won a competition with one of those shots and later he'd given Billy a poster-size blowup of the winning entry—a doe with her fawn. Billy had loved the picture.

Taking a deep, steadying breath, Tanner slowly turned around. The poster was still hanging above the bed. Though a little tattered at the corners, it was a breathtaking shot and one of Tanner's all-time favorites.

Crossing to the bed, Tanner sat down and kicked off his shoes. He relaxed against the pillows, stretching his legs on top of the old threadbare bedspread.

With his hands clasped behind his head, Tanner scanned the room once more, noting with a sigh the numerous postcards pinned to the corkboard on the opposite wall—postcards he'd sent Billy from practically every city in Europe.

Not much of a letter writer, the postcards had been Tanner's way of keeping in touch with his younger brother. But had he known then that they were to become a source of conflict between Billy and Mac and ultimately himself and Mac, he might have thought twice about sending them.

And judging by the reception he'd received on the jetty and again downstairs, reestablishing a relationship with his father wasn't going to be easy. Not that he'd expected it to be.

But at the moment all that mattered was that he was home...and home to stay. In his travels he'd seen some of the most beautiful scenery in the world, but as far as he was concerned there was nowhere more scenic, nowhere as breathtakingly beautiful and nowhere he'd rather be than Moonbeam Lake.

He was tired of hopping from one country to another, one continent to another; tired of living out of a suitcase with no place to call home.

Mac was all the family he had left in the world, and Tanner was determined that the wall of resistance Mac had constructed could and would be breached.

Suddenly Tanner found his thoughts switching to the moment when he'd stepped out of the car and glanced toward the jetty. For an electrifying second he'd thought fate was handing him a gift, and that before him was Leanne, the woman who'd haunted his dreams for the past six years.

His whole body had tensed and a feeling of excitement had tugged at his insides. But the moment she'd looked over her shoulder at him, he'd realized he was mistaken, and the feeling of disappointment that followed had had the impact of a blow to the solar plexus.

He remembered now that Laura and Leanne were cousins, and no doubt the family resemblance and the fact that he hadn't seen either of them since that summer six years ago was reason enough for him to have been momentarily fooled.

Leanne was a year older and much more outgoing than Laura. Over a period of years both girls had worked at the resort during their summer vacations. Laura had always been shy and reticent, while Leanne liked to be noticed and liked to flirt. Though he'd tried to keep their relationship platonic, her interest in him had been blatant at times.

But on the night of Billy's death, Leanne had shown a side of herself he'd never seen before. He was almost sure he'd never have made it through the hours of darkness and despair without her.

Several days had passed before he'd had a chance to go and see her, only to be told by her mother that she'd left for the mainland with no mention of when she'd return.

That their encounter had obviously meant very little to her had come as something of a blow both to his ego and his senses. On reflection, her going shouldn't have surprised him... and yet...

With a tired sigh Tanner closed his eyes and deliberately turned his thoughts to the present, to the problem facing him now. Somehow he had to make his father see that it was time to put the past behind them, that they were still a family and while Billy's death had been a cruel twist of fate, no one had been at fault....

"He's asleep. I told you." A child's voice drifted through to Tanner and he stirred from his slumber.

"Are you sure?" another voice asked.

"His eyes are closed. He must be asleep." The first voice spoke again.

Tanner slowly opened his eyes and found himself being stared at by two children. For a fleeting moment he couldn't remember where he was, but as they continued to stare at him, recognition and remembrance came flooding back.

"Are you awake?" Craig asked him.

"I think so," Tanner replied, easing himself into a sitting position.

"Carly wanted to ask you if you're really Mac's son, like Mom said," the boy continued, his tone serious.

Tanner glanced at Carly, whose blue eyes were fixed on him. "Yes, I'm Mac's son," he told her, wondering as he spoke to the child why there was something vaguely familiar about her.

"See, I told you," Craig said to his sister.

"But you're not a kid," Carly accused him, holding his gaze.

"No," Tanner said, noting with amusement the look of disappointment in the depths of Carly's beautiful blue eyes. "I'm sorry." Tanner felt the need to apologize.

"Come on, Bro." Carly headed to the door.

"Don't tell my mom we were here, okay?" Craig said as he began to follow his sister.

"Why not?" Tanner asked, curious now.

"'Cause she told us not to bother you," he explained.

"Bother me any time you like, I don't mind. Besides, I was a kid once, you know," he added, wanting to redeem himself in some way.

"You were?" Craig said disbelievingly, and at his words Carly halted in the doorway and turned around.

"Sure," he went on. "I'll even show you a photograph," he offered, refraining to mention that the picture was one of Billy at the age of five, on his first day of school.

"Okay," Craig said.

Tanner slid off the bed and crossed to the dresser where the photograph of Billy usually sat.

"There's a picture right here, somewhere," Tanner said, frowning as he scanned first the top of the dresser, then the shelves of the bookcase. It didn't take him long to realize that the photograph was gone, along with every other picture of Billy.

"Carly! Craig! Are you upstairs?" Laura called from the foot of the stairs. As usual they'd helped her set the tables in the dining room, but after gobbling down their own supper in the kitchen they'd done their disappearing act.

She'd cautioned them not to bother Tanner, to steer clear of him. Perhaps she was overreacting, but she hadn't recovered from the shock of seeing him again and she was at a loss to know what to do. His arrival had thrown her for a loop and her first reaction, to grab the twins and leave, was as powerful now as it had been the moment she'd heard his voice that afternoon on the jetty.

What if he noticed the resemblance between himself and the children? What if he became suspicious and started asking questions? What if the conversation should turn to the night of Billy's death and Mac mentioned that on the night of Tanner's arrival home, Leanne and Billy had talked Laura into switching identities to see if Tanner would notice?

Laura put a brake on her galloping thoughts. After all this time it was unlikely Mac even remembered, so much had happened that night.

"Carly! Craig! Where are you?" Laura turned her attention back to the children, but there was no answer and before she could follow her instincts and head upstairs, the telephone rang. With a sigh she turned and crossed to the reservations desk.

* * *

When he'd heard Laura call out to the twins, Tanner had almost responded, but one glance at their anxious faces had changed his mind.

"Quick, let's go down the back stairs," Craig said after peeking around the edge of the door. Giving his sister a nudge into the hallway, he turned to Tanner. "Bye." He waved and with a grin was gone.

"Bye," Tanner replied and chuckled softly to himself as he watched them race headlong down the hall toward the back stairs that led down to the sunroom. Shaking his head he returned to the task of locating the picture.

Tanner ran a hand through his hair and frowned. Mac had to have taken all the photographs from Billy's room and put them away, he reasoned. They had to be in the attic. That's where Mac had put the photographs of his wife after she died.

It had been several weeks after his mother's death that Tanner had noticed that every picture of her had been taken down. At first he'd thought Mac had destroyed them, but after searching the house over a period of several days, he'd finally located them in a storage box in the attic.

Obviously Mac had put Billy's photographs there, too, thought Tanner. While he was tempted to go to the attic and confirm his suspicion, he decided to wait. If he was to make any progress at all with Mac, he'd have to move slowly, take one day at a time. And bringing out pictures of Billy wasn't the place to start.

Lifting his suitcase onto the bed, Tanner extracted his shaving kit and a clean shirt, and headed for the bathroom. As he waited for the sink to fill, his thoughts turned to the twins, wondering fleetingly if their father was from around here and if he knew him.

Whoever the man was, he was lucky to have two such beautiful children. Twins—what a fascinating photographic subject they'd make, he thought as he stripped off his shirt.

He'd never considered using children as subjects before. But the more he thought about the twins the more intrigued he became.

Besides, there was something about those two—especially Carly—that seemed familiar. She reminded him of someone. But who? It would come to him in time, he thought as he bent to scoop water into his hands.

He splashed his head and neck several times and after lathering the soap, began to wash his face.

Suddenly there was a knock at the bathroom door, then another, more urgent this time. Blindly Tanner reached for the towel on the rail and wiping the soap from his eyes, he opened the door.

"Oh...hello, Carly," Tanner said, flipping the towel over his shoulder.

Carly didn't answer, but simply dropped her chin to her chest and began to fidget.

"Oh...ah...you want to..." Tanner began, quickly guessing the reason for Carly's agitation. "Go ahead," he told her. "I'll wait out here." He stepped into the hall.

Carly didn't need a second invitation. Rushing inside, she slammed the bathroom door.

A loud rumble of thunder reverberated above her as Laura made her way up the back stairs. She'd popped her head into the games room to check on the twins and found Craig watching two older boys, who were stay-

ing with their parents in one of the cabins, playing video
games. When she'd asked him where his sister was, he'd
shrugged his shoulders and said he didn't know.

Afraid that her inquisitive daughter might have decided to ignore her instructions to stay away from Tanner, Laura made her way to the second floor. While
Craig tended to ask questions, Carly preferred to explore and observe, those big cornflower-blue eyes of
hers missing nothing. And that was the problem,
thought Laura—those big blue eyes of Carly's were so
like Tanner's. How long would it be before he noticed
the resemblance and started asking questions?

Laura felt her heart skip a beat at the prospect of
Tanner uncovering the truth. During the past hour
while she'd been busy serving the evening meal to those
campers renting the cabins, her mind had been trying to
come up with a solution to her dilemma.

She'd thought of telling Mac that she had to go back
to Vancouver because of a family emergency, but she
knew she couldn't lie to him any more than she could
leave him in the lurch without a cook.

The fact that she hadn't seen Tanner at all during the
past hour had had her wondering if he'd changed his
mind about staying, but that faint hope had been
dashed when she'd glanced outside and seen his car still
parked in front of the lodge.

Suddenly Laura heard a door slam. The culprit could
only be Carly. Ever since someone had walked in on her
the first day they'd arrived, Carly had resorted to
slamming the door as a means of informing anyone
nearby that the bathroom was occupied.

Laura ran up the remaining steps to the landing and
came to an abrupt halt at the sight of Tanner, naked to
the waist, standing in the hall outside the bathroom.

Every nerve in her body jolted to life and her mouth went dry as her gaze traveled over his tanned muscular frame. His face was hidden from view in the soft folds of a towel, and for a moment, at least, he was unaware of her scrutiny.

Her eyes were instantly drawn to the sprinkling of dark hairs that covered his chest and continued down to disappear beneath the belt of his jeans. Alarm bells sounded in her head, her skin began to tingle and a heat slowly spread through her, bringing a soft moan of pain and denial to her lips.

She bit down on her lower lip to stifle the sound as Tanner lifted his head and met her gaze. Laura felt her heartbeat pick up speed, drumming against her rib cage like the rain hammering on the roof above them.

"Are you looking for Carly, by any chance?" he asked, as he casually draped the towel around his neck.

Laura drew a steadying breath. "Yes," she said, keeping her distance, willing her heart to slow down.

"She's in the bathroom," he told her. "I think it was an emergency."

"With Carly it always is," Laura replied, relieved that her voice gave no indication of the turmoil raging within her. "She always waits until the very last minute."

The bathroom door opened and Carly appeared. "There is another bathroom downstairs," Laura reminded her daughter.

"But I had to go..." Carly said moving toward her mother.

"I'm sorry," Laura began.

"No problem," Tanner assured her. "Ah...I must have dozed off. Is my father around?"

"Mac went out a little while ago to check on the cabins and the campers, to see if anyone needs anything," she told him as she took Carly's hand.

"What's the forecast?" he asked, and in answer to his question another loud rumble of thunder sounded above them.

"According to the radio there's a second storm front moving in bringing gusty winds and rain, but it should be gone again by morning."

"Maybe I should go and see if Mac needs help securing the boats," he added, starting to turn away. "By the way, I didn't notice any teenage kids around when I drove up. How many did he hire this summer?" He eyed Laura inquiringly.

"He didn't hire any."

"You have to be joking!" Tanner exclaimed.

"I'm not," Laura replied. "He told me all the teenagers say the money isn't good enough."

"But he can't run this place by himself. It's too much, even for him," Tanner said.

"I know," she agreed. "And I've told him that, on numerous occasions."

"What about your husband? Isn't he working here, too?"

Laura blinked in surprise at the question and felt her pulse accelerate. "No," she managed to say and quickly dropped her gaze.

"Does he work in town?" Tanner asked.

This time Laura felt her face grow hot. She stooped to pick up Carly, careful to avoid Tanner's gaze. "No," Laura replied, fighting down the panic that was threatening to take hold. "Excuse me, but I've got work to do downstairs." Without waiting for a reply, she turned and headed for the stairs.

"Mommy, what's a husband?" Carly asked when they reached the bottom of the stairs. Laura darted a glance back the way she'd come, praying silently that Tanner hadn't heard Carly's question.

"A husband," she repeated softly as she set Carly down, and crouched beside her. "Well a husband is...ah...when a man and woman get married, the man is called the husband and the woman is his wife," she explained.

Carly was silent for a long moment, a thoughtful expression on her pretty face. "You mean like Mr. Lee and Mrs. Lee?" she asked.

"Yes, that's right," said Laura with a brief smile. The Lees owned the corner grocery store a block from her apartment in Vancouver. They worked together in the store and were very friendly toward the children, always greeting them with a warm smile.

"Your brother is in the games room," Laura said. "Run and tell him it's almost bath time."

"Can we call Grandma tonight?" Carly asked.

"We could. Why?"

"I miss her," Carly said. "When is she going to visit us?"

"Why don't you ask her when we call?" Laura suggested as she stood up.

"Okay." Carly said cheerfully, before scampering off to find Craig.

Laura entered the kitchen and as the swinging door closed behind her, she found her thoughts returning to the encounter with Tanner on the landing. The image of him standing naked to the waist flashed into her mind and immediately she felt her heart pick up speed.

She'd almost forgotten how beautiful he was, how incredibly male and how dangerously attractive. Eyes that glittered like sapphires and a face etched with strength and determination. A face that had haunted her dreams for too long. And there was an aura of confidence about him, a hint of arrogance, that gave him an added dimension, and set him apart from every other man she'd ever met.

Not that she'd known many men in her life, she thought, with a shake of her head. Her father had walked away from his wife and daughter shortly after Laura was born. As a result of his desertion, Laura's mother had had to work doubly hard raising her daughter on her own.

Shy and withdrawn as a child, Laura had grown up feeling awkward and uncomfortable around boys and men, while her cousin Leanne had been an outgoing child and a precocious teenager.

Laura and Leanne were opposites in personality, but a good deal alike in appearance. Both had had shoulder-length chocolate-brown hair and gray-green eyes. But while Laura had a few more freckles on her face and lips that were fuller, Leanne's figure was definitely more curvaceous. The fact that their mothers were twins was undoubtedly the reason they looked alike.

Laura was almost thirteen the year she and her mother moved to Vancouver and that was the summer Laura began spending her school vacations with her aunt and uncle and cousin at their cabin at Moonbeam Lake.

Although Leanne was a year older than Laura, they hit it off famously, and it wasn't long before Laura began telling Leanne she wished she could be more like her.

She'd hardly finished saying the words when a mischievous gleam came into Leanne's eyes. That's when she'd suggested they switch places; pretend to be each other. Wouldn't it be fun to trick everyone? she'd said.

Laura hadn't seen it that way at all, but after much coaxing from Leanne she'd agreed to try to see if they could fool her aunt and uncle.

They'd traded clothes and combed their hair in the same style and to Laura's astonishment they'd fooled her aunt and uncle as Leanne had predicted. But when her cousin suggested they trade places for a day and see if they could fool everyone at the resort, Laura had refused, reluctant to continue the deception.

Over the years Leanne had periodically attempted to coerce Laura into trading identities, just for fun, but Laura had always refused...until that fateful night when she was eighteen.

Laura sighed. Many times over the past six years she wished she'd never let Billy and Leanne talk her into playing a part in the ploy to see if Tanner could tell the cousins apart.

But they'd both been aware of the crush Laura had on Tanner and the fact that this might be the last summer she would spend at the lake and therefore her last chance to make him notice her.

Whatever her reasons for agreeing to the scheme, it had set into motion consequences she could never have foreseen. The deception had backfired, and Laura had paid dearly for what had essentially been a simple prank.

Suddenly a flash of lightning splintered across the sky, instantly diverting Laura's thoughts from Tanner and to the figure crouching over one of the rowboats on the jetty.

It had to be Mac, Laura thought, and she could see he was attempting to tie the boat more securely to its moorings. Seconds later a crack of thunder, much louder than any that had come before, resounded through the air. She flinched, her eyes closing momentarily in reaction. When she opened them, she was in time to see Mac keel over and disappear into the lake.

One moment he was there, the next he was gone!. Somehow he must have fallen in! Spinning on her heels Laura raced to the door only to collide with a figure coming from the opposite direction.

"Oh!"

"Sorry!" Tanner said, as he grabbed Laura's arm to steady her.

"Tanner! Hurry! It's your father...he's fallen into the lake," Laura said, her voice steadily rising in fear and panic.

"What?" Alarmed, Tanner stared down at her.

"Just now... I saw him..." Laura sputtered, unable to get the words out fast enough. "Tanner! We have to help him," she practically shouted at him.

Tanner heard the note of fear in Laura's voice and immediately released his hold on her. He raced to the door and was through it and running toward the jetty in a matter of seconds. Rain lashed at his face and the wind buffeted his body, slowing his steps and making it difficult for him to see.

Above him the sky was black and though it was only seven in the evening, the dark cloud cover made it seem much later.

Reaching the wooden jetty, Tanner quickly scanned the water between the boats, wiping his face every few seconds in order to clear his vision.

Suddenly he caught a glimpse of a head and shoulders, and an arm waving in the water. Without a thought to his own safety he dived in. Surfacing clear of the boats, he searched the water in front of him. With deft movements he swirled around and found himself face-to-face with his father.

The old lifesaving skills he'd thought were long forgotten sprang to mind and he immediately moved behind Mac, grabbing him under his arm and across his chest, lifting his head out of the water. "Don't struggle! I've got you!" Tanner yelled into his father's ear, and to his relief Mac obeyed.

With a quick glance over his shoulder, Tanner saw Laura and immediately he began to kick in her direction.

Laura knelt on the jetty and watched anxiously as Tanner pulled his father through the water toward her. Somehow Tanner managed to bring Mac alongside, enabling Laura to reach out and grab on to him.

"Hang...on to him...until I...get out," Tanner ordered, his words coming out in gasps.

Laura nodded and clung tightly to Mac and in a matter of seconds Tanner was beside her and together they hauled Mac onto the jetty.

"How's he doing?" Tanner asked as he bent his head close to his father's face and checked his breathing.

Laura glanced at Tanner and their eyes met and held for one intense second, just long enough for her to see the glimmer of fear lurking in the depths of his eyes.

Suddenly Mac started to cough and sputter and Laura saw the look of relief that crossed Tanner's taut features.

Mac moaned and coughed again, effectively drawing Laura's attention away from Tanner. Though Mac's face was pale, his eyes were clear and he managed a weak smile.

"My knee hurts," Mac said in a hoarse voice.

"We'd better get you up to the house," Tanner said.

"And out of those wet clothes," Laura replied as a rumble of thunder sounded in the distance. "You, too!" she said, turning to Tanner.

"Right! Let's go!" Tanner said. With his arm around his father he lifted Mac. Laura scrambled to her feet, put her arm around Mac's waist, and the threesome headed for the lodge.

Throughout the short journey, all Laura could think about was that if Tanner hadn't been there to pull his father out of the water, Mac could quite easily have drowned.

Chapter Three

As they reached the lodge, a small group of anxious campers came to meet them. The twins stood in the doorway, and seeing their frightened expressions Laura flashed a reassuring smile in their direction.

"Mac's going to be all right," she told the children as the group moved aside to let them pass.

"I'll take him up to his room and get him out of his wet clothes," Tanner said, once they were inside. "Laura, call Doc Morro and ask him if he'll drive over and take a look at Mac."

"I don't need a doctor," Mac mumbled, but Laura noted the paleness and lines of pain on his face and glancing at Tanner she nodded in silent acknowledgement of his request.

"Here, I'll give you a hand." The offer came from Phil Smith, one of the campers renting a cabin on the beach.

"Mommy, did Mac fall in the water?" Craig asked as he and his sister followed Laura to the telephone.

Forgetting the telephone for a moment, Laura crouched to the children's level. Carly's eyes were glistening with tears and Laura put an arm around each child. "Mac slipped and fell into the lake," she explained calmly. "But Tanner jumped in and pulled him out."

"You mean Mac could have drownded?" Craig asked, his eyes wide.

Laura saw Carly's lower lip was beginning to tremble and gently she stroked her daughter's hair. "Yes, Mac could have drowned." She spoke quietly and composedly, not wanting to frighten the children. "But he didn't. Tanner saved him."

"Wow!" Craig said, his eyes bright with excitement. "Just like a superhero," continued the boy, who was an ardent fan of comic book and movie heroes.

"Yes, just like a superhero," Laura agreed, thinking that Craig's comment was apt indeed.

"Will Mac be all right?" The question came from Carly who'd been listening intently.

"Yes, I'm sure he'll be fine." Laura spoke with confidence and at her words she felt her daughter relax. "Tanner wants me to call the doctor so he can come and give Mac a checkup just to make sure," she went on. "It would be a big help to me if the two of you would go to your room and get ready for bed. We'll skip bath time tonight."

"What about Grandma?" Carly asked. "Can we still call her?"

"We'll see," Laura said, and at her words a look of disappointment appeared on Carly's face. "I have to call the doctor for Mac first." Both children nodded in understanding. Laura smiled and gave them a brief hug before standing up. "Off you go, and don't forget to brush your teeth." As they moved to do her bidding, she reached for the phone. Locating the doctor's number, she began to dial.

Tanner shivered uncontrollably as he lowered his father onto the wicker chair next to the bed. Mac was shivering, too, and ignoring his own discomfort, Tanner began to pull off his father's wet jacket.

During the summer months the water temperature near the shore was usually warm enough for swimming. That, and the fact Mac hadn't been in the water too long was a definite plus.

In all likelihood he'd suffer no ill effects after his unscheduled dip, but as Tanner tugged his father's jacket free and began to unbutton Mac's shirt, he couldn't erase from his mind the look of fear he'd seen on Mac's face.

"I'm quite capable of undressing myself. I'm not a child," Mac muttered, and hearing the note of exasperation in his father's voice Tanner immediately released his hold on the shirt.

"Take off the rest of your wet things and I'll get you a towel," Tanner ordered as he turned and hurried from the room. He returned moments later with two large bath towels he'd found in the bathroom.

Mac hadn't moved. He sat in the chair, his head in his hands.

"Darned knee..."

"Are you all right?" Tanner asked, his shoes squelching noisily on the hardwood floor as he crossed to the chair.

"I'm fine," Mac said through clenched teeth, and Tanner heard the pain in his father's voice.

"Did you say your knee hurts?" Tanner asked as he threw the towel around Mac's shoulders.

"It's nothing," Mac said adamantly, but Tanner wasn't convinced. After much cursing from both parties, the rest of Mac's clothes were finally removed. Then, pulling back the bedcovers, Tanner eased Mac onto the bed.

"Get under the blankets," Tanner ordered. "With any luck the doctor should be on his way."

"Dr. Morro said he'll be here as soon as he can," Laura said as she came to a halt in the doorway. She'd stopped off at her room for a minute and changed out of her wet clothes and into a warm fleecy jogging suit. "Is there anything I can do?"

"I don't need a doctor, dammit!" grumbled Mac. "I'll be fine."

"For heaven's sake, man! You could have drowned out there," Tanner exclaimed in disbelief.

"Nonsense!" Mac replied. "I'm here, aren't I?"

Laura noted that he deliberately avoided looking at his son. "There's no need for all this fuss..." Mac went on. "Call the doctor back and tell him not to bother. I'll be as good as new in the morning."

"I don't believe this!" Tanner said, dragging his fingers through his wet hair in a gesture of frustration. "In a minute you'll be telling me that I didn't need to jump in and haul you out...that you were quite capable of getting to shore on your own." His words were dripping with sarcasm.

Mac plucked at the bedcovers with nervous fingers, continuing to avoid Tanner's scathing gaze. "It wasn't as bad as it looked—" he began.

"Like hell!" Tanner cut in, and Laura could feel the anger coming from him in waves.

Though she was surprised at Mac's reaction, she sensed that he was finding it difficult dealing with the fact that the son he'd banished from his home, the son he'd sworn he never wanted to see again had saved his life.

"You are a stubborn—" Tanner began, then broke off abruptly, anger and frustration in every line of his body.

The tension in the air was almost palpable and Laura was afraid that the two men would end up yelling at each other, possibly saying things they'd later regret and so she quickly intervened.

"Tanner, why don't you go and get out of those wet things?" she suggested, keeping her tone light.

Instantly Tanner's gaze swung to meet hers. His eyes had darkened to an iridescent blue and as their glances collided, the air between them crackled with tension... and something more. Laura felt her heart kick against her rib cage in a response she could neither ignore nor control, but she held his gaze, keeping his attention away from Mac and the all-out confrontation that appeared imminent.

She watched as Tanner drew a steadying breath. "You're absolutely right," he said at last, filling the uneasy silence. As he spoke, Laura was aware of an almost imperceptible relaxing of his expression, as well as the glint of understanding in his eyes. "Tell Doc I'd like to see him before he leaves," Tanner added as he turned and left the room.

Laura released the breath she hadn't known she'd been holding and looked toward the bed. "Mac..." she said softly, a hint of reprimand in her voice.

"Don't *you* start on me," Mac replied gruffly as he pulled the towel around his shoulders.

"He *did* pull you out of the water, you know," she went on evenly as she crossed to the bed.

She heard him sigh. "I know." His words were a mere whisper of sound. "I don't understand...why he didn't just leave me there," he added, dropping his face into his hands.

"Mac, don't..." Laura began, but before she could say more she heard the sound of voices in the hallway, and moments later a man in his mid-fifties appeared in the doorway of Mac's bedroom.

"Mac McLeod! What's this I hear about you going for a swim with your clothes on and in this weather?" The man flashed Laura a smile as he approached Mac. Setting his bag on the end of the bed, he snapped open the lock.

"Dr. Morro, I'm Laura Matthews," she introduced herself. "Mac was tying up the boats when he fell in. Fortunately he wasn't in the water too long."

"*You* didn't pull him out, did you?" the doctor asked as he thrust a thermometer into Mac's mouth and reached into his bag once more for his stethoscope and blood pressure kit.

"No, Tanner did," Laura said.

"Tanner!" The doctor's surprise was evident in his voice. "Well, well! I didn't know he was coming home this summer." He busied himself with wrapping the blood pressure pad around Mac's upper arm. "When did he arrive?"

"This afternoon," Laura replied.

"His timing couldn't have been better, then." The doctor chuckled. "And you, young woman... You look familiar," he continued in the same jovial tone. "I do know you, don't I? Didn't your folks own that cabin farther along the beach?" he asked as he removed the thermometer from Mac's mouth and studied it.

"No, that was my aunt and uncle," Laura told him as a shiver of apprehension raced across her skin. She glanced toward the bedroom door, relieved that there was no sign of Tanner.

She wanted to steer clear of the subject of her aunt and uncle and cousin, especially around Tanner. And she didn't want to trigger any memories in Mac, either, in case he inadvertently said something that would make Tanner suspicious and start asking questions.

"All right, Mac, tell me what happened out there," Dr. Morro said. "How did you manage to fall in? Did you hit your head or hurt yourself on one of the boats when you fell?"

"It happened so fast," Mac said with a shake of his head. "There's a loose board on the jetty I've been meaning to fix for a while now. I think I must have caught the toe of my shoe on it. Something wrenched my knee and the next thing I knew I was in the water."

"I'll check your blood pressure, then I'll take a look at your knee."

"If you'll excuse me Dr. Morro, I'll leave you to it." Laura crossed to the door. "Ah . . . by the way, Tanner would like to talk to you before you leave," she added.

"Good! I'd like to have a chat with him, too," the doctor replied.

Laura nodded and hurried down the hall to the twins' room. She could see that the door was ajar and as she drew near she heard her son's voice. "But superheroes always wear capes," she heard him say and Laura smiled as she pushed the door open.

"Are we all ready for bed?" she asked brightly, but the sight of Tanner sitting on Craig's bed brought her to an abrupt halt.

He'd changed into a pale blue sweater and gray jogging pants and appeared relaxed and none the worse for his brief ordeal in the water.

"These two are certainly dressed for bed," Tanner said in a light tone. "But I'm afraid I don't have my jammies on, yet." He gave Laura a heart-stopping grin.

Both Craig and Carly started to giggle at his words, but when Tanner glanced at Laura, a look he couldn't quite define flashed briefly in the depths of her gray-green eyes.

Puzzled, he continued to study her, wondering fleetingly how he could have mistaken her for Leanne that morning. Laura's hair, still damp from the rain, was a rich dark chocolate color and cut to just below her chin. Expertly styled, it curled attractively against her slender neck.

And while Laura's eyes were similar to Leanne's, they were more green than gray and there was a hint of mystery as well as a quiet maturity and wisdom in their depths.

Tanner felt his heart stumble before picking up speed and he was astounded to discover it was Laura he was reacting to—shy, quiet . . . stunningly beautiful Laura.

Silently he reminded himself she was a married woman with two children, two children who simply by their presence had magically made the anger he'd felt at his father dissipate like a puff of smoke.

"Do you have cartoons on your jammies, too?" Carly asked, effectively capturing everyone's attention.

Tanner laughed, a low seductive sound that sent a tingle of awareness chasing along Laura's nerve endings. The last thing she'd expected when she'd entered the twins' bedroom was to find Tanner there. He'd been in a foul temper when he'd stormed from Mac's bedroom—and he'd had every right to be—but obviously a change of clothes had done wonders to restore his good humor.

"No, my jammies don't have cartoons on them," he said evenly. "But I bet your daddy has jammies just like yours." At his words, he was surprised to see the children's smiles vanish and their glances dart to their mother.

The silence was unmistakably tense. Something was wrong... he could feel it.

Panic and fear mingled to momentarily paralyze Laura and for several long seconds she couldn't think of a thing to say.

"We don't have a daddy," said Craig, his tone matter-of-fact and void of emotion.

Tanner threw a startled glance at Laura, noting the anxious expression on her face as well as the pain that shone briefly in her eyes. He felt like a fool. It was his own fault, of course. Because she had children, he'd simply assumed she was married. And assumed, too, that her husband was working close by or in town.

He supposed he was old-fashioned enough to believe that being married and having children went hand in hand... but that wasn't always the case.

On reflection, Laura had never said a word to confirm his assumptions. In fact, she'd shied away from the questions he'd posed about where her husband worked. And she didn't wear a ring.

He should have picked up on that. But he'd had other things on this mind and as a result he'd blundered, and blundered badly as it was obvious from her reaction as well as the twins', that the subject of their father was taboo.

"I'm sorry..." he began.

"It's okay." Laura lied. "You didn't know," she added, wishing he would leave, wanting to avoid having to answer any questions, though she doubted he'd ask in front of the children.

Suddenly the sound of Dr. Morro's voice reached them. "I'll come back and see you tomorrow, Mac," he was saying, and Tanner immediately rose from the bed.

"I'd better go and talk to Lou," he said, and Laura nodded. "Good night, you two." His voice was soft as he gave the children a smile.

"'Night," they replied in unison.

There was silence for several seconds after Tanner left and as Laura gazed down at her children, she felt a warm rush of love for the two of them. Never for a moment during the past six years had she had any regrets about the choices she'd made.

Carly and Craig were the most important people in her life, and she would do anything, even lie, to protect them.

"Let's read a story," Laura suggested, and immediately the children relaxed and the usual argument about which story she would read quickly ensued.

Carly, as always, chose "Cinderella," while Craig, who preferred stories about animals or stories with more excitement, chose "Peter and the Wolf."

In the end Laura read both "Cinderella" and "Peter and the Wolf." After kissing the twins good-night and promising Carly that they would call Grandma Irene the following evening, she quietly closed their bedroom door.

Laura walked down the hall to Mac's bedroom. The door was ajar and she knocked quietly but there was no answer. Peeking around the edge of the doorway and seeing that Mac was sleeping, she withdrew and made her way downstairs.

She found Tanner and Dr. Morro in the dining room and they both stood as she entered.

"Would you like a cup of coffee?" she asked.

"Not for me, thanks," the doctor replied.

"How's Mac?" she asked, motioning them to sit down.

"I was just telling Tanner that Mac's knee is swollen a little, but I'm more concerned about his blood pressure." Dr. Morro's tone was serious.

"Thanks," Laura said as Tanner pulled another chair up to the table where they were sitting. "His blood pressure?" she repeated as she sat down next to Tanner.

"Yes," the doctor said. "I've been trying to get Mac to come in for a physical for the past few years, but every time I'd mention it, he'd pooh-pooh the idea and insist he was fine."

"And he's not?" Laura asked, glancing at Tanner and seeing the concern on his face.

"No, he's not," Dr. Morro confirmed. "His blood pressure is elevated. I'm going to put him on medication—though if I know Mac, he'll just shove the pills into a drawer and ignore them."

"Give them to me. I'll make sure he takes them," Laura said.

"Taking the pills isn't enough," the doctor continued. "Mac needs to slow down . . . to take it easy." He smiled assuringly. "Don't look so worried. He's only seventy-one, and other than his blood pressure being a little high, he's in good shape."

"How do we get him to slow down?" Tanner asked and at his reference to "we" Laura felt her heart skip a beat.

"I think the swelling on his knee will keep him in bed for a few days at least," Dr. Morro said. "And in the meantime, you can try talking some sense into him."

"Laura was telling me Mac hasn't hired any summer help this year," Tanner said.

"He hasn't hired anyone, other than kitchen help, for the past few summers," the doctor said. "Mind you, from what I can gather, business has dropped off a bit . . . but it's been the same everywhere. Still, the general maintenance and upkeep of a place like this is . . . Well, it's constant and Mac's been doing all that work himself."

"Thanks, Lou—I already feel guilty enough," Tanner said, pushing his chair away from the table and rising to his feet.

"Tell me it's none of my business," Dr. Morro said, "but why have you stayed away so long?"

"It's none of your business," Tanner said, more than a hint of anger in his tone.

Laura could feel the tension emanating from the man standing beside her. Instinctively she reached out and put a hand on his arm to soothe him.

The moment her hand touched his, a jolt of sensation, much like a small electric charge, scampered up her arm. Astonished, she withdrew her hand immediately, thankful that Tanner was too caught up in his own emotions to notice her reaction.

Dr. Morro laughed and shook his head. "Like father, like son." His tone was wryly affectionate.

"What the hell does that mean?" Tanner asked, his anger in full evidence now.

"Hold your horses!" Dr. Morro cautioned. "You and your father are a lot alike, you know. You're both stubborn and you go off the deep end at the drop of a hat. I suppose that's why you tend to rub each other the wrong way."

"Tell me about it." Tanner sighed. "And in case you're interested, I haven't exactly ignored my father these past six years. I called him every Christmas, and sent letters, which he never bothered to answer...." Tanner's voice trailed off and Laura felt her heart go out to him.

"Your father never was very good at showing his softer side," the doctor said. "Your mother was the only one I knew who could bring it out in him. Well, this is getting us nowhere." He, too, got to his feet. "I better head on home. I haven't heard any thunder for a while and it sounds like the rain has eased up, too."

"Thanks for coming by so promptly," Laura said.

"No problem. I'll drop in again tomorrow and see how he's doing. I'll have a prescription filled and bring his blood pressure medication with me," Dr. Morro added as he walked toward the door.

"I'll see you out," Tanner offered.

"Nice to have met you, Dr. Morro," Laura said to the departing figure.

"You, too." The doctor nodded to Laura as he and Tanner left the room.

Laura returned the chairs to their proper places and crossed to the swinging door leading into the kitchen. Her mind was still on the comments Tanner had made.

Somehow the knowledge that he had kept in touch with his father throughout the past six years made her feel warm inside.

But the warmth was fleeting and followed swiftly by feelings of guilt . . . guilt concerning her decision not to contact Tanner five and a half years ago to inform him she was pregnant. She'd acted with her head and not her heart, but she really hadn't had much choice. By the time she realized she was pregnant, Tanner was in another country, on another continent.

She could still vividly recall the first time she'd ever set eyes on Tanner. It was the summer she'd turned thirteen and she'd come to Moonbeam Late to stay with her aunt and uncle at their cabin.

Leanne had taken her on a walk to explore the area. They'd wandered along a well-trodden path that led through a patch of trees and down to the lakeshore. As they'd walked toward the lake, they'd heard loud voices as well as the sound of people splashing in the water.

When they emerged from the trees, there were a group of young guys swimming in the lake. Most of them looked to be about their age or older.

At fourteen, Leanne was very boy-conscious. She'd just finished telling Laura about a boy at high school she liked and at the sight of these young men Leanne's face had lit up like a neon sign.

Laura remembered feeling embarrassed as they'd walked toward the group and she'd suggested to Leanne that they turn back. But her cousin had ignored her, much more interested in finding out exactly who this group of guys were.

At her high school in Vancouver Laura had often listened to some of the older girls talking about boys, describing in great detail how their pulses would race at the sight of one particular boy; or how their legs would feel weak if that boy should actually look their way; or how their skin would tingle if they accidentally brushed against him.

Laura had always found their comments laughable until the moment that she'd watched Tanner walk out of the water and into her life.

Her lungs had suddenly forgotten how to function and her heart had jacknifed inside her breast before galloping on like a mad thing. Her legs had felt like two sticks of wet spaghetti, almost giving out beneath her.

She'd never seen a man in such a state of undress before, nor had she ever seen such a magnificent male body, and for the first time in her life she experienced the array of sensations she'd once scoffed at . . . but no longer.

How young and naive she'd been, she thought with a tired sigh. She'd dreamed of Tanner every night that summer and all through the school year that followed, longing for another summer to arrive so that she could see him again.

"Laura?" Tanner's voice startled Laura and a shiver of awareness rippled through her.

"Yes," she managed, though she didn't turn around.

"Would you mind very much if I helped myself to something from the fridge?" he asked. "I missed supper and I don't think I could make it till morning without a bite to eat."

Laura turned to face him. "I'm sorry. That's my fault. I should have sent one of the twins to wake you," she said apologetically.

"Don't worry about it," Tanner said.

"There's lots of leftover fried chicken and potato salad." Laura tried to ignore the way her pulse had picked up speed at the sight of him.

"Look, don't let me keep you from anything," he said.

"The twins are already asleep," she told him. "I was just going to make myself a cup of tea."

"You make the tea. I'll raid the fridge," he said and followed his words with a quick grin.

"Sure." Laura turned back to the counter, wishing his grin wasn't so disarming, or his presence quite so overwhelming.

"It's certainly been an eventful evening," Tanner commented.

"To say the least," Laura replied as she started getting things ready for tea, thinking all the while he didn't know the half of it.

"I was certainly surprised to see you here," Tanner said as he carried several dishes from the fridge to the table by the window.

"No more surprised than I was to see you." Laura began to think she should have made her escape while she'd had the chance.

"Someone mentioned that you and your mother bought a restaurant in Vancouver a couple of years ago."

"We did," Laura said, and a prickle of apprehension danced across her skin as Tanner lifted his eyes to meet hers.

"Now I'm really puzzled," Tanner said. "Tell me, Laura, if you have a restaurant in Vancouver, why *did* you take on the job as cook for my father this summer?"

Chapter Four

Laura turned on the faucet and as the kettle filled with water, she was glad of the few seconds respite before she had to supply an answer.

Setting the kettle on the gas stove, she glanced toward Tanner, to see him gently closing the refrigerator door with his foot.

In one hand he carried the large bowl of leftover potato salad and in the other, a plate with several pieces of chicken.

He crossed to the table and set the food down and Laura automatically reached for the cutlery drawer and extracted a knife and fork.

Moving toward the table, she held them out to Tanner. "Thanks," he murmured, taking the utensils from her, and as his fingers made fleeting contact with hers, a thrilling sensation shimmied along her nerve endings, and it was all she could do not to snatch her hand away.

She felt her face grow warm in response and was relieved that Tanner had already turned away, too preoccupied to notice. Laura retreated to the sink and with her back to him now, she busied herself setting two cups and saucers, a sugar bowl and cream jug on a tray.

Reluctantly she joined him at the table and he lifted his dark head to flash her a smile as she set down the tray.

"You haven't answered my question," he said lightly. "What brings you here?"

His blue eyes, so like Carly's, held hers and for an astonishing moment Laura found herself on the brink of blurting out the truth. She quickly controlled the wildly foolish impulse, and to give herself a few extra seconds, she spun away and returned a moment later.

"I forgot spoons," she said somewhat lamely as she held up the utensils. Keeping her eyes averted, she pulled out the chair across from him and sat. "There's not much to tell," she began. "I heard through a friend that your father needed a cook for the summer and... Well, I thought the children would enjoy spending time here." Her explanation came to a halt.

"What about your restaurant? How's business? Aren't you the chef there, too?" he asked between bites.

"Business is doing well," she told him truthfully and not without a hint of pride. "Thanks to our location, we do a steady lunch trade. That, together with a growing evening trade, keeps us busy. We even had to hire an assistant chef a few months ago," Laura said.

"That's terrific." Tanner's tone was sincere. "But I still don't understand why you'd want to cook here for the summer."

The kettle on the stove began to whistle and, thankful for the distraction, Laura rose from the chair and crossed to the counter. "Things are much more relaxed here," she said as she dropped several tea bags into the teapot. "I can spend time with the children during the day as well as experiment with new recipes or fine-tune some old tried-and-true ones," she explained.

"I see," Tanner said, then he smiled. "And do the campers who come to the resort know they're really guinea pigs?" he teased.

Laura felt a rush of pleasure in response to his smile. "I won't tell if you won't tell," she countered, trying with difficulty to match her tone to his.

Tanner lifted a chicken leg from the plate. "All I can say is, if this is a sample of what you've been dishing up at mealtimes around here, no one will ever want to leave." He gave a contented sigh. "This is absolutely delicious," he added, before taking another bite.

Being complimented on her cooking was nothing new for Laura, but somehow no comment had ever meant more. "Thank you," she managed to say as she poured tea into the cups.

"Who looks after the twins while you're at the restaurant?" Tanner asked between mouthfuls.

At this question Laura felt a moment of panic. She hesitated just long enough to draw a questioning glance from Tanner. She drew a steadying breath. "My mother and I managed to organize our schedules so that one of us is always with them," she explained. "Can I get you anything else?" she asked as she handed him a teacup.

"No, thank you. This is fine," Tanner said, faintly puzzled at the pause and the hint of nervousness he'd detected in her voice. It was apparent Laura was somewhat sensitive when it came to discussing the twins. He hoped she didn't think he was being intrusive, but he couldn't help wondering why she was so reticent, and wondering, too, about how she'd come to be a single parent.

He hadn't really been prying. Or at least he didn't think so. He'd simply been curious about whether or not she placed the twins in daycare while she worked as many parents chose to do. He didn't think his question had been out of line—nor indeed the comment he'd made earlier concerning their father.

But he remembered that Laura had always been a rather private person and he supposed that was reason enough for her to be hesitant when anyone asked questions about the twins. Yet he couldn't quite dismiss the notion that there was a lot she wasn't telling him.

"So what brings *you* back?" Laura asked, hoping to steer Tanner away from the subject of the twins.

She watched as an expression she couldn't quite define flitted across his handsome features.

"I've stayed away too long, much too long," he said at last and Laura heard the regret in his voice. "I decided it was time I came home and made peace with my father, and myself," he went on, a hint of determination underlying his words. "Though Mac's reception wasn't all that welcoming." He gave Laura a rueful smile.

"I must admit your father did look a bit surprised," Laura said, recalling the shock she'd seen in Mac's eyes when Tanner had arrived that afternoon. "But I don't think he's as angry as he pretends to be. Just give him time."

Tanner sighed, leaned back in the chair and stared into space. "I've heard that before, but I hope you're right," he said with heartfelt emotion. "I can't tell you how many times during the past six years I've wanted to drop everything and get on a plane and come home."

"Why didn't you?" she asked, unable to stop herself.

Tanner abruptly brought his eyes back to Laura and for several long seconds she was held prisoner by his relentless gaze.

"I'm sorry," Laura said quickly, beginning to feel uncomfortable under his scrutiny. "It's really none of my business."

"No. It's all right," Tanner said evenly. "I've asked myself that question a hundred times." He leaned toward her, resting his forearms on the table. Bowing his head he studied his hands. "I think the answer is that I couldn't bear the thought that Billy wouldn't be here...." He broke off and there was no mistaking the pain in his voice.

Laura's hand was halfway to Tanner's bent head before she hastily withdrew it. She ached for him and her instinctive reaction was to offer comfort, but she quickly reminded herself that that was also all she'd set out to do when she'd come upon Tanner staring out over the lake, prostrate with grief the night Billy died.

Suddenly Tanner pushed the chair back and got to his feet. Turning away he began to pace. "Laura ... Look, I'm sorry..."

"Don't be," she quickly assured him as she rose and put away the food before gathering up Tanner's plate and her own cup and saucer from the table.

"Billy always said you were a good listener," Tanner continued.

At his words Laura felt a stab of pain and regret. Fearful she'd drop the dishes, she carefully placed them in the sink before turning to Tanner. "He did?"

Tanner nodded. "Every summer when I came home, he'd talk about you and your cousin. He thought very highly of you. He often told me he could talk to you about anything. Oh . . . and speaking of your cousin, what's Leanne up to these days?''

Though his question sounded casual enough, Laura noted the tension in his features as he waited for her reply.

"She lives in Hawaii," Laura said, and at her words she saw a flicker of disappointment cross his features.

"Really?" Tanner replied. "If that's the case, I don't suppose you see her very often."

"No," Laura said as she began washing the dishes in the sink. "She flies into Vancouver, usually without warning, once or twice a year."

"Hawaii? What does she do there?" Tanner asked, picking up the dish towel from the counter. "Is she married?"

Laura bit back a sigh and tried to ignore the pain that clenched her heart at Tanner's obvious interest in Leanne. "She owns a boutique in one of the shopping malls," Laura said. "She was married, but she's going through a divorce."

"A divorce," Tanner repeated thoughtfully.

Suddenly her head began to throb. "I'm rather tired. I think I'll finish these in the morning," she said softly as she turned off the tap and reached for the hand towel, wishing all the while that the subject of Leanne had never been brought up.

"Does my father still do a final walk around before going to bed?" Tanner asked.

"Oh . . . yes . . . I forgot . . ." Laura said.

"I'll take care of it," Tanner quickly assured her.

Laura nodded. "He'll appreciate that. Well, I'll say good night," she added, and after a mere flash of a smile she was gone.

Tanner listened to the sound of her footsteps on the wooden floor as she crossed to the stairs and made her ascent. He smiled to himself as the silence settled around him and a feeling of nostalgia tugged at his heart.

Thoughtfully, he finished the task of washing the dishes, setting them on the drain board to dry, and as he made his way outside to check the grounds, he couldn't recall ever talking to Laura on a one-to-one basis, or in such depth before.

What he found surprising was that he'd felt totally at ease with her, and though it hadn't been his intention to tell her the reason he'd stayed away, somehow telling Laura had been both easy and strangely healing.

Billy had been right. She was a good listener. He smiled as he pictured her in his mind's eye—hair the color of rich, dark coffee and eyes that at times looked green and at other times gray. Her skin was lightly tanned and free of makeup and her lips were full and sensual—infinitely kissable. He shook his head. In any event, the fact that she'd listened without commenting, without making a judgment and without trying to tell him she knew exactly how he felt, was not only refreshing but unusual.

Tanner lingered on the porch and let his glance travel down to the jetty where the boats were bobbing gently on the water. The storm had abated but the night sky was covered with dark clouds that hid the moon.

As he began to make his way around the lodge, his thoughts shifted to those happy days when he'd return to the lake to spend a month with his father and brother, helping out during the resort's busy summer season.

Any spare time he'd had, he'd spend with Billy, swimming or fishing, hiking or sailing. Suddenly memories of those summers filled Tanner's mind and he braced himself for the heartrending pain that usually accompanied these moments.

But the pain didn't come this time. Instead, he felt a deep sense of sorrow, and another emotion he couldn't quite define, leaving Tanner with the strong conviction that his decision to return to Moonbeam Lake had indeed been the right one. His healing had begun.

Laura lay on her bed staring up at the shadows on the ceiling. She heard the sound of footsteps on the stairs and knew it was Tanner returning from his inspection of the grounds. As he entered the bedroom next to hers, she held her breath and listened to the muted sounds he made as he prepared for bed.

She heard the bedsprings groan under his weight, and slowly released the breath she'd been holding, trying not to think about how close he was, or how he might look with that long, lean body of his stretched out on the bed.

A shiver danced across her skin and silently Laura admonished herself for the direction her thoughts had taken, but she found it impossible not to think of Tanner and Billy and that summer so long ago.

She and Billy had indeed been friends and confidants. He'd confided in her his dreams of seeing the world, seeing the places on the postcards Tanner sent him, while she in turn had told Billy of her dream to own a restaurant.

Though she'd never told Billy about the feelings she had for his older, handsome brother, he'd guessed, and he'd teased her every chance he got.

The summer Billy died was the summer they'd both turned eighteen, and on the day Tanner was due to arrive, Billy was relentless in his teasing. He told her that as this was possibly her last summer at Moonbeam Lake she'd have to do something drastic to make Tanner notice her.

That's when Leanne, who'd been eavesdropping, jumped into the fray commenting that if Laura dressed more femininely, and was a little more outgoing, even flirted with Tanner, she might make some headway.

Billy's immediate comment was that Laura should simply take a leaf out of Leanne's book.

As soon as the words left Billy's mouth, his eyes lit up and before she could blink, he threw out the challenge that she trade places with Leanne and see if Tanner could spot the change.

Laura wasn't eager to comply, but Leanne and Billy wore down her resistance, bullying her into giving it a try, just as a joke.

Reluctantly she subjected herself to Leanne's ministrations which, once completed, made her wish she'd never agreed to participate at all. Though once in the minidress she was surprised by how much she did look like her cousin, Laura felt sure Tanner would know immediately that she was an imposter.

Tanner arrived that same afternoon just before dinner, and less than an hour later she heard Mac, Billy and Tanner talking loudly in the kitchen. She knew Billy had planned to tell his father about his proposed trip to Europe, as well as the fact that he'd already bought his ticket, and she felt sure that this was the subject under discussion.

The argument continued for some time and she had to forgo her nightly chore of resetting the tables in the dining room for breakfast. Instead, she retreated outside where she ran into Leanne who was waiting for a lift into town to see a movie.

Laura declined her cousin's invitation to join her, saying she still had the kitchen to clean up, and after Leanne departed, Laura lingered by the jetty, her concern mainly for Billy.

But a few minutes later Billy stormed out of the lodge, driving off in his car in a cloud of dust. She'd approached the lodge only to hear Mac and Tanner still arguing. Unwilling to intrude yet anxious about the outcome Laura decided to wait.

It seemed like only a short time later that a police car pulled up and two policemen emerged. Their knock brought an end to the raised voices inside, and when the officers haltingly told the news that Billy had run his car into the concrete abutment near the railroad tracks and been killed outright, their words were met with a stunned, and disbelieving silence.

Shocked, Laura could only stand in the shadows hardly able to believe what she'd heard.

It was very late when Mac and Tanner returned from the hospital where they'd been taken to identify Billy. Laura was sitting on the porch hugging her knees, letting the tears fall.

Neither Mac nor Tanner noticed her, but she was instantly aware of the tension between them, a tension that erupted in a fresh argument the moment they were inside the lodge.

Mac made no bones about the fact that he blamed Tanner for the accident; that Billy would never have wanted to leave home and travel around Europe if Tanner hadn't sent him the postcards and filled his head with dreams.

That Mac was beside himself with grief was all too clear, and Laura could only listen as Mac's tirade went on and on and Tanner stood silently waiting for him to finish.

When Tanner suddenly pushed open the screen door and hurried past her, she heard the sounds of sobbing coming from inside. But when she went to him Mac gruffly brushed aside her comforting words before heading upstairs.

Laura ran outside and in the shadowed darkness she saw Tanner's figure striding purposefully along the lake shore. The stretch of land where Laura found him was a fair distance from the lodge, and at two o'clock in the morning only the moon and stars were out.

"Beat it, Leanne!" Tanner yelled. "Just leave me alone."

That he thought she was Leanne was undoubtedly due to the fact that she was still wearing the body-hugging minidress that belonged to her cousin. Too caught up in the dramatic events unfolding she hadn't thought to go back to her cabin to change.

But as Laura turned to obey Tanner's directive, her footsteps faltered and she slowed to a halt. Instead of leaving, she lowered herself onto a rock nearby and sat waiting. Tanner told her a second time to leave, but his tone was unconvincing and so she remained where she was.

He began to pace, berating himself out loud for not trying to stop Billy when he'd stormed out. Her heart aching with love, Laura simply listened to him vent the emotions raging inside him, the disbelief, the denial, the anger and the pain.

When at last he lapsed into silence, Laura glanced toward him and thought her heart would break when she saw him drop onto the ground in a gesture of total despair.

She rose and crossed to where he sat on a soft bed of moss, holding his head in his hands. She knelt in front of him and in a move that was solely meant to comfort, she reached out and put her hands on his shoulders.

At her touch he lifted his head and when she saw the tears shimmering in the depths of his eyes, her only thought was to try to ease his anguish.

"Tanner, don't do this to yourself," she said in a husky voice.

Tanner gazed at her for a long moment before answering. "Leanne, my father believes Billy is dead because of me." His voice was rife with emotion.

"Mac is just lashing out, Tanner," she said, her words a mere whisper, but Tanner didn't seem to hear her.

"I wish it had been *me* in the car instead of Billy," he said almost inaudibly.

"Don't! Don't say that." Laura wanted to shake him out of the torment he was feeling.

Tanner blinked and met her gaze. "I do believe you're the only one who seems to care that *I'm* hurting, too," he said. "Thank you." He lifted his hand and gently brushed her cheek in a feather-light caress.

At his touch a shiver of awareness danced across Laura's skin, creating a strange excitement deep within her. Their glances collided and the air between them suddenly seemed to crackle. Laura couldn't think or breathe as his blue eyes held hers captive in a look that touched her very soul.

She felt his hand slide along her neck, his fingers delicately entwining themselves in her hair. Slowly, tentatively, he drew her to him. When he was only a matter of inches away he stopped, almost as if he was giving her the opportunity to escape, but seconds later, when his mouth touched hers, escape was the furthest thing from her mind.

A need, stronger and more powerful than anything she'd ever felt before tore through her, igniting a fire that raged with a speed that was frightening.

His tongue plunged deeper into her mouth, becoming entangled with her own in an enticing, erotic dance of desire. There was an urgency in him, a driving force that she responded to with all her heart.

Suddenly she was in the center of the conflagration, racing toward the heat, clinging to Tanner, as though he were a lifeline.

So this was desire, she thought hazily as his hands began an exploration that made her blood sing and her skin tremble.

With every breath, every touch, every kiss, she was driven to a frenzy of need, a need only he could appease. The sweet smell of moss mingled with the earthy male scent of the man who was taking her on a journey of discovery.

When she felt the soft bed of moss press against her naked back, she was so hot she thought she might explode. And when at last their bodies were joined, the brief flash of pain she felt was instantly forgotten, lost in the incredible sensations. Higher and higher they flew until together, they touched the sky.

Laura sat bolt upright in bed shaken by the strength of her memories. Her heart was pounding and her cotton nightgown was clinging to her body. A long-forgotten ache tugged instantly at her lower regions and she covered her mouth with her hand, afraid for a moment that she'd cried out. But the house was eerily silent with only the faint sound of the wind rustling through the trees outside.

Minutes passed and she felt her heartbeat slowly begin to return to normal, and drawing her knees up she hugged them to her in an attempt to ease the torment still raging within.

Tanner had only been home a matter of hours and already he was wreaking havoc with her emotions and her senses. For the past six years she had deliberately kept the memory of that magical night locked securely away.

His arrival at the lodge had clearly undermined her resolve and lowered her guard and though there was only six weeks of the summer season left, she had the feeling they might well be the longest and most challenging six weeks of her life.

Chapter Five

Laura had spent a restless night and was in the kitchen brewing a large pot of coffee earlier than usual. After throwing together the ingredients for the next batch of muffins, she put them in the oven, then carrying a breakfast tray of cereal and fresh fruit, coffee and bran muffins, she made her way upstairs to Mac's room.

Since she knew him to be an early riser she was certain Mac would be anxious and impatient to be out of bed. She knocked softly.

"Yes! Who is it?" came the disgruntled response.

Laura entered and shook her head when she saw Mac, still dressed in his pajamas, sitting on the edge of the bed. His face was pale and it was obvious he was in pain.

"You're not thinking of getting up, are you?" Laura asked, and at her words Mac threw her an angry glance.

"Of course, I'm getting up. I certainly can't stay in bed all day. There's too much work to be done," he told her in no uncertain terms.

"But Dr. Morro..."

"Hang Doc Morro," retorted Mac. "There's nothing wrong with my knee," he told her, and as if to prove his claim he stood up. The grunt of pain that erupted from him startled Laura and she quickly set the tray on the old pine hope chest at the foot of the bed and moved to his side.

"Mac," she cautioned as she gently urged him down onto the bed. "You'll only do more damage if you try to get up." She eased his legs onto the bed. "Why don't you just relax and enjoy," she said as she tucked in the covers and plumped up his pillows. "I wouldn't mind a couple of days in bed and a little pampering myself." She flashed a teasing smile.

"Relax and enjoy, she says," Mac grumbled, as Laura moved to the foot of the bed to retrieve the breakfast tray.

"Don't you like having breakfast in bed?" She set the tray across his lap.

"Who's going to look after things around here? Who's going to do my chores? That's what I'd like to know," Mac continued to complain.

"I will, of course."

At the sound of Tanner's deep resonant tone Laura felt her stomach contract and her gaze flew to the man standing in the doorway.

Pale blue jeans hugged legs that were long and muscular and a white cotton T-shirt accentuated his broad shoulders and athletic build. His hair, still damp and slicked back from his face, threw his features into sharp relief.

A shiver of awareness chased along her nerve endings, sending messages to her brain she tried hard to ignore. It was all she could do to drag her eyes away from Tanner and back to Mac.

"There, see? Everything's under control. You don't have to worry," she told Mac in an overly bright tone.

"I just came from the jetty," Tanner said, stepping farther into the room. "A few eager beavers have been out on the lake since dawn," he said. "One fellow on the jetty was asking me what kind of bait he should use..."

"A willow leaf with a speckled green fly is what they're biting these days. But some of the trout aren't fussy at all, and anything and everything seems to work," Mac said. "One of Jack Bishop's kids caught a three pounder offshore just the other day, and he was using worms." He paused, his face creasing in a thoughtful frown. "That's something I was planning to do today—dig up a fresh batch of worms from the compost."

"I'll take care of it," Tanner said. "I came to ask if you still followed the same routine, or if there's anything I need to know."

Eager to make her escape, Laura jumped in. "Well, if you'll excuse me, I left some muffins in the oven," she said, gradually backing away. "Enjoy your breakfast. I'll be back for the tray later."

Laura came to a halt outside the twins' room and took a deep steadying breath. She was annoyed with herself for the way she'd reacted to Tanner. After all, she wasn't a starry-eyed teenager any longer, she was a mature woman of twenty-four and the mother of twins.

Quietly she opened the bedroom door and peeked inside, smiling at the sight of the twins still asleep in their beds. Closing the door again she continued downstairs and busied herself in the kitchen mixing the ingredients for a batch of banana bran muffins.

When the timer on the oven began to buzz she slid her hands into oven gloves and extracted the two trays of muffins from the rack. Turning, she suddenly found herself staring at Tanner who'd just entered the kitchen.

"Those smell good," he said with a smile. "And a large mug of coffee would go down a treat, too," he added, crossing to the counter.

"Help yourself," Laura said as she set the trays on the counter to cool.

"May I help myself to a muffin?" Tanner asked and Laura practically jumped out of her skin when she realized he was standing directly behind her.

Reaching over her shoulder he chose a muffin from the ones already cooling and bit into it. "Mmm . . ." he commented before devouring the rest of it. With a cheeky grin he leaned forward and reached for another, and this time as he withdrew he brought his face close to hers, an action that played havoc with her senses.

"These are delicious," he murmured, his breath fanning her face, sending shivers down her spine. "And you smell rather nice, too."

Laura had to close her eyes against the onslaught of emotions erupting within her. Her legs felt like pieces of straw and she had to lean on the counter to stop herself from falling.

She sensed rather than saw him move away and she opened her eyes, relieved to discover that he was at the far end of the counter pouring coffee into a mug.

"Mommy! What's for breakfast? We're hungry," the twins chorused as they entered the kitchen.

Startled, Laura turned to greet her children and couldn't stop the smile that curled at her mouth as she crouched down beside them.

They'd dressed in a hurry, that much was obvious. Craig wore a pair of blue shorts and a green T-shirt that was inside out. Carly also wore shorts but hers were green and the purple T-shirt she'd chosen was half-on and half-off. Craig, always quicker than his sister, had finished dressing first and not wanting to be left behind, Carly had abandoned the job midstream.

"Did you two dress yourselves?" The question came from Tanner and Laura heard the amusement in his voice.

The twins were nodding vigorously and Laura was about to throw Tanner a cautionary glance in the hope of cutting off the criticism she felt sure was coming, but she was already too late. "Well, all I can say is you both did a great job," Tanner said and at his words Laura flashed him a grateful smile.

Gazing down at Laura crouched beside the twins Tanner felt his pulse pick up speed at the sight of her smile. Suddenly he found himself wishing he had his camera in his hand, wanting to capture the smiles on all of their faces.

It struck him again that Laura had grown into a beautiful young woman, a warm and caring person who quite openly adored her children. Tanner found himself thinking wistfully that he'd gladly give his eyeteeth for kids of his own, and acknowledged that that was another reason why he'd returned home. He wanted to settle down, to raise a family of his own.

In his travels around the world he'd met a number of women, and he'd dated a few, but the fact that he'd never stayed in one place had made it impossible to establish a long-term relationship.

One day he hoped to find a woman with whom he could share his hopes and dreams, a woman with whom he could spend the rest of his life.

"Can we have pancakes today?" Craig's question, addressed to his mother, cut through Tanner's wayward thoughts, bringing him back to the present.

"Maybe after breakfast you and your sister could give me a hand digging for worms," Tanner suggested.

Craig's eyes lit up and he quickly turned to his mother. "Can we, Mom? Can we?" he asked, assuming his role as spokesperson for the duo.

Laura hesitated, not altogether sure it was a good idea for the children to spend time with Tanner, but the eager expressions on Craig's and Carly's faces were difficult to ignore. She had no real reason to refuse Tanner's offer and she'd come to appreciate the fact that Mac took the children off her hands most mornings allowing her to accomplish a great deal of work.

"It's very kind of you," she began. "But are you sure?" she asked, wondering if he realized what he was getting into.

"Absetively," he replied with a confident smile.

"Is that a yes?" Craig asked.

Tanner nodded. "Meet me out on the porch when you're finished breakfast. I have a couple of things I want to take care of first." He topped up his mug with coffee and headed for the door.

Impatient to be off, the twins opted for cold cereal with the fresh strawberries they'd helped Mac pick the morning before. They bolted down their breakfast and left the table in record time.

"Hey... maybe the two of you could pop in and see Mac later," she said as they headed for the door. "After you've finished digging for worms, I mean..."

"Okay," Craig said. "Bye, Mom," the twins chorused before racing out to the porch.

Laura gathered their dishes and returned to the sink, watching through the kitchen window as Tanner greeted them. He crouched to their level and began talking earnestly to the twosome.

Seeing them with their heads close together Laura suddenly tensed as she was struck by the resemblance between Tanner and the children. Surely he would notice, she thought with growing panic.

But what could she do? She couldn't run out and grab the twins and tell them she'd changed her mind about their spending time with him. Perhaps the resemblance was only obvious to her, she rationalized. When she'd first arrived she'd worried that Mac might comment on the children's likeness to Tanner, but he hadn't seemed to notice, either. She would just have to stay calm and take things one day at a time.

Laura continued to watch as Tanner handed Craig a small shovel and Carly an empty ice-cream container. As the three of them headed toward the end of the lodge Laura could barely see for the tears in her eyes and she had a lump in her throat the size of a baseball.

Giving herself a small shake, she reminded herself that she didn't have time to worry about whether or not she should have sent the twins off with Tanner. She had work to do, but first she poured a fresh mug of coffee for Mac and headed up the stairs.

"More coffee?" she asked as she entered his bedroom. "How about another muffin, more toast?" She was pleased to note that he'd eaten everything she'd brought earlier.

"No, coffee's just fine, thanks Laura," Mac said.

"I'm heading out to clean up cabins one and two. The Uelands and the Ulmers are arriving this afternoon," she reminded him.

"Right," he acknowledged. "They're nice families, they come every year."

"Can I get you anything before I go?" she asked as she picked up the tray.

"No...I...are the twins going with you? If you don't want them underfoot they can stay here with me," he suggested and Laura heard the love for the twins in his voice and sensed that he missed their company.

"Actually, they've gone with Tanner." A look of disappointment crossed his features. "They've gone to dig for worms," she explained. "They shouldn't be long. I told them to come up and see you when they get back."

Mac nodded and smoothed the covers on the bed with his hands. "You're very lucky, Laura," he said softly. "They're great kids. I'm going to miss all three of you when the summer's over."

At Mac's words Laura suddenly found herself blinking back tears. "We'll miss you, too, Mac," she managed to say. "Well, I'd better get cracking." She stopped in the doorway. "I trust you won't do anything stupid while I'm gone, like try to get up?"

Blue eyes met hers. "Believe me, if I could I'd be out of here like a shot," he grumbled, good-naturedly. "I'll be fine. Off you go," he assured her with a wave of his hand.

Laura went downstairs, put the dishes in the sink and after collecting the cleaning kit from the cupboard in the kitchen, headed along the trail to the first cabin on the edge the lake.

After Laura had finished cleaning cabins one and two she made her way back to the lodge. The day was bright and sunny and the jetty looked bare with most of the boats out on the lake. Several young children were playing in the cordoned-off area near the shore that was safe for swimming, their parents sitting on the sandy beach keeping an eye on them.

Laura waved at them in greeting before opening the screen door and going inside. She wondered for a moment where Tanner and the twins were but when she heard the sound of children's laughter coming from the floor above, her question was instantly answered.

Putting the cleaning kit away Laura quickly got together some sandwiches for lunch, then ran upstairs to find Craig and Carly seated on the foot of the bed playing Go Fish with Mac.

"How's it going in here?" she asked, strangely relieved that there was no sign of Tanner.

Mac looked up at her and smiled. "Apart from the fact that these two are beating me hands down, everything's just fine."

"Did you find lots of worms?" she asked the children.

Carly turned to her mother, eyes bright, her smile wide. "Tanner gave me a baby shovel and I dug some worms all by myself," she said with evident pride.

"I used a *real* shovel," Craig said, not wanting to be outdone. "We found a whole bunch of worms and Tanner said if it's okay with you, he'd take us fishing this afternoon so we can try the worms ourselves. And Mac says he thinks the trout like worms best," he finished breathlessly.

"Well . . ." Laura began, a little overwhelmed at the enthusiasm in Craig's voice and surprised, too by how animated Carly had been.

"Is this a private party, or can anyone join in?"

Laura felt her pulse accelerate as Tanner appeared in the doorway behind her.

"This isn't a party," Carly said with a giggle. "You're supposed to have balloons and a clown at a party."

Tanner laughed, a deep rich sound that sent tremors racing through Laura.

"I'll try to remember that," he said, amusement lingering in his voice. "Did you ask your mother about your going fishing with me later?"

"Yes," Craig said, throwing a pleading glance at Laura.

"What did she say?" Tanner asked.

"I didn't say anything," Laura replied.

"I've never seen two kids take to fishing the way these two have," Mac said, joining the conversation. He glanced up at Tanner. "They remind me of you and Billy—" Mac abruptly broke off, a startled expression on his face as if the mention of Billy's name had surprised him.

"Who's Billy?" Craig wanted to know, effectively diverting everyone's attention.

Tanner took a deep breath before answering. "Billy was my brother," he said evenly.

"Do you still go fishing with Billy?" Craig asked, oblivious to the tension simmering in the room.

Laura almost groaned aloud, wishing her son wasn't quite so inquisitive.

"No," Tanner replied with a brief hesitation. "Billy died in an accident." He kept his explanation simple, and glancing at Mac, Laura saw tears gather in the older man's eyes.

"Grandma Irene says that when you die you go to heaven. So he must be in heaven," Carly said with a logic that was difficult to dispute.

"That's right," Tanner said softly, feeling strangely comforted by the child's words.

"Don't you miss him?" Once again Craig made his presence known and at the words Tanner felt a pain clutch at his heart.

"Craig, I think you've asked enough questions."

Tanner heard Laura gently scold her son, and was about to intervene when his father spoke.

"We miss Billy very much." There was no mistaking the emotion in his voice.

Tanner felt as if the breath had been knocked from his body. He threw his father a startled glance, surprised that he'd used "we" and not "I." For a heart-stopping moment he saw a reflection of his own pain and sorrow in the depths of his father's eyes. For the first time in six years Mac was actually sharing his feelings with Tanner, including him, in a way he'd never done before.

Laura caught the look that flashed between Tanner and his father and sensed that though Mac might argue the fact, he'd just taken the first step toward a reconciliation with his son.

"Come on, you two." Laura crossed to the bed to scoop Carly into her arms. "If you want to go fishing later you'd better come and give me a hand in the kitchen now."

"You mean we can go fishing with Tanner?" Craig asked as he hopped off the bed.

"Yes," replied Laura. "But first you have to help me wash the vegetables for supper."

"Oh, Mom, do we have to?" Craig said glumly as he followed his mother from the room.

Laura had merely wanted to leave Tanner and Mac alone for a while in the hope that they might continue to talk about Billy. Since her arrival more than a month ago she'd never heard Mac mention either son and she felt sure that simply the fact that he'd spoken about Billy, and in Tanner's presence, was a breakthrough.

"What's for lunch? I'm starving," Tanner's voice cut through her thoughts a few minutes later when he joined them in the kitchen.

"The sandwiches are already made," Laura said, glad that her voice betrayed none of her inner tension. "There's cold meat, lettuce and tomato on a bun and what's left of the potato salad." She pointed at the dishes on the counter nearby, wishing she could control her reaction to this man.

"I'm washing the carrots," Carly said, smiling up at Tanner as she dunked a carrot into the basin of luke-warm water on the table in front of her.

"Can I help?" Tanner asked.

"Sure," Craig said.

"Okay," Carly replied. "You can sit next to me if you like. Here's some carrots."

"And broccoli," Craig said.

Laura continued to stir the iced tea, surprised to hear her daughter's invitation. Shyer than her brother, Carly generally took her time getting to know someone, and it was usually several days before she relaxed and started talking. Tanner, however, seemed to have won her over in a matter of hours and Laura wasn't quite sure how she felt about that.

The sound of a car's tires on the gravel outside caught her attention. "Dr. Morro's here," she announced. "I think I'll put a couple of sandwiches on a plate and if the good doctor hasn't eaten he and Mac can have lunch together."

"Good idea," Tanner said. "We're finished washing the veggies." He lifted the basin of water and carried it to the sink. "Who wants a sandwich?"

"I do. I do," came the chorus.

As Laura left the kitchen, a plate of sandwiches and two glasses of iced tea on the tray, she tried not to think about the twins' happy smiles as Tanner served them their lunch.

She told herself that she shouldn't feel upset that they appeared to like him. He was their father, after all. Her annoyance quickly gave way to feelings of guilt. It was obvious from the way he treated the children that he'd make a wonderful father and she found herself wondering again if she had made the right decision by not telling Tanner about the twins.

But, she quickly reminded herself, the night Tanner had made love to her, the night she became pregnant, he'd thought he was making love to her cousin Leanne. And by the time she realized she was carrying his baby he was already thousands of miles away in Australia.

"Ah . . . perfect timing I see," Dr. Morro said with a smile, as he opened the screen door and spotted Laura with the tray.

"Indeed you have," Laura replied, pushing aside her wayward thoughts.

"How is my patient today?" the doctor asked as he shifted his black bag from one hand to the other.

"I think he's resigned himself to the fact that he'll be holed up in bed for a few days."

"Good," came the reply. "Do you want me to carry that, or can you manage?"

"I can manage," Laura said as she climbed the stairs ahead of him. "You have a visitor," she told Mac as she crossed to deposit the tray on his lap. Turning to the doctor once more she added. "Stop by the kitchen before you go."

As Laura descended the stairs she heard the sound of laughter coming from the kitchen. Pushing open the swinging door she was met with a sight that stopped her in her tracks. Craig was hanging from one of Tanner's arms and Carly from the other. Tanner, in turn, was lifting the children off the floor, alternately raising and lowering them to the floor.

The muscles across Tanner's upper body and arms were straining from the exertion, but he seemed unaffected by the obvious effort and strength involved. The twins, of course, were squealing with delight and pleading for more.

"What on earth..." Laura began, dragging her gaze away from Tanner's rippling muscles.

Glancing up, Tanner immediately stopped the game, setting the children gently on their feet.

"We were playing yo-yo," Carly said, grinning from ear to ear and still clinging to Tanner's hand.

"Yo-yo," she repeated with a shake of her head.

"Tanner was showing us what a yo-yo does," Craig explained.

"I see, I think," Laura said, wondering why she suddenly had the urge to pull the children from Tanner's grasp and into her arms. "Why don't you two finish eating lunch, and remember, before you can go anywhere, and that includes fishing, you have to tidy up the games room for me," she added as she crossed to the sink.

"Oh, Mom," the twins said in unison.

"No arguments, please," she cautioned, and no doubt hearing the note of authority in her voice the twins immediately returned to the table.

Tanner had been silent since she'd entered the kitchen and Laura could feel his gaze on her now. She tried with difficulty to ignore him. She wasn't quite sure why she was pulling rank—no, that wasn't strictly true, she amended thoughtfully.

The stab of jealousy she'd experienced on seeing the twins having such a wonderful time with Tanner had caught her off guard and her reaction, to put a stop to the fun, had simply been instinctive.

From the time the twins had been born she'd tried to be both mother and father to them. While their grandmother, Irene, deserved some credit, Laura was proud of the way she'd raised the children, proud that she'd accomplished so much on her own.

And she wanted things to stay that way, she told herself resolutely. But if that was true, then why had she come back to Moonbeam Lake? The question came unbidden into her head. Because she wanted the children to get to know their grandfather, she told herself calmly. That was all.

But was it? a small voice inside her head persisted in asking. Hadn't she really come back to Moonbeam Lake in the hope that she might indeed meet Tanner again?

"No!" She didn't realise that she'd spoken the denial aloud until Tanner spoke.

"No what?" he queried, coming up behind her.

"Oh... nothing, I was just thinking out loud," she said, confusion and embarrassment sending a rush of color to her cheeks.

"Thanks for lunch." Tanner noted the blush on her cheeks and wondered what had caused it. "I don't suppose you'd like to come fishing with us, would you?" he added on impulse, thinking that perhaps she'd had plans to spend time with the children herself that afternoon, and he'd interfered by offering to take them fishing.

Surprised and warmed by the invitation, she hesitated, but only for a moment. "No... thank you," she said. "I have supper to prepare and there's those new arrivals this afternoon. With Mac out of commission I'd like to be on hand—" She broke off, hoping she didn't sound as if she was simply making excuses.

"Maybe I should stay..." Tanner began.

"No, you go ahead," Laura urged, and was relieved when he didn't argue.

Just then, Dr. Morro appeared, carrying the empty tray. He told them about the medication he'd left for Mac, and the fact that Mac had grudgingly promised to take the prescribed pills.

Laura ushered the twins to the games room and helped them tidy up the newspapers and comic books which had been left lying around.

When they returned to the kitchen Tanner was already out on the porch and there was no sign of the doctor. She located the children's life jackets, and in short order they were off to the jetty with Tanner.

Laura spent the remainder of the afternoon making several fruit pies, experimenting with different pastry recipes. It was much too hot to bake, but Laura was determined to keep busy. She also made a number of small meat pies which she planned to freeze for future use.

She was interrupted twice, once when the families renting the two cabins arrived and a second time when she took Mac a glass of lemonade.

After checking on Mac and finding him dozing she'd quietly gone to her room, and feeling hot and sticky, she'd opted for a quick shower, hoping she'd be finished before the children and Tanner returned.

The cool water felt wonderfully refreshing and Laura lingered under the spray longer than she'd planned as thoughts of Tanner filled her mind. When she found her fantasies getting out of hand she abruptly turned off the water and drew aside the shower curtain. Before she could make a move toward the towel hanging on the towel rail, the bathroom door was suddenly flung open and Carly ran in.

On the landing, a few feet behind Carly was Tanner. His blue eyes widened with shock when he saw her, before his gaze lifted to lock on hers. Lightning arched between them for a split second before Carly, in her inimitable fashion, slammed the bathroom door.

Paralyzed by the drumming of her heartbeat, Laura couldn't move or think. Her whole body began to tremble and reaching out she hauled the towel off the rail and quickly wrapped it around herself.

"Carly!" The child's name came out in a throaty whisper and not an angry reprimand as she'd hoped.

"What?" Carly asked, gazing up at Laura, totally unaware of what had just happened.

"How many times have I told you that if the bathroom door is shut, you should knock first?" Laura asked.

"But I knew it was you," came the prompt reply.

Laura opened her mouth to give Carly a lecture, but stopped herself, knowing it was futile. "Did you catch any fish?" she asked instead.

"Nope," Carly said, but there was no hint of disappointment in her voice. "Tanner showed us all the places where he and his brother Billy used to go fishing. He let me and Craig take a turn steering the boat, too. That was neat. Can we go with him again tomorrow?"

"Ah . . . well, I guess we'll have to see," Laura said. "I thought we might go for a walk and take a picnic with us."

"Can Tanner come?" Carly immediately wanted to know. "He knows lots of trails. He told us."

Laura tried to keep the irritation she felt out of her voice. "Tanner might be busy," she said casually.

"I'll ask him," Carly said, and with that she was out of the bathroom before Laura could stop her.

Chapter Six

As Laura dried herself with the towel, she mumbled under her breath in frustration, wishing she hadn't mentioned the possibility of a picnic to Carly. Pulling on her robe Laura tentatively peeked out into the hallway, relieved to note it was empty.

Scurrying to the safety of her bedroom she deliberately took her time getting dressed. She ignored the sleeveless summer dress she'd planned to wear and pulled on a pair of white cotton pedal pushers and a short-sleeved red cotton blouse.

After drying her hair, she lingered in her room as long as she could, trying unsuccessfully to convince herself that she really wasn't hiding. But every time she thought of Tanner and that shattering moment when their eyes had met, a shiver of awareness chased across her skin and a yearning she'd long since forgotten tugged at her.

How could she face him? The question kept popping into her head and her stomach churned at the prospect of seeing him. But she couldn't stay in her room indefinitely. She had too much to do.

Resolving to act as if nothing had happened, Laura closed her bedroom door and hearing laughter coming from Mac's room headed in that direction, silently saying a prayer.

Her prayer was answered. Tanner was nowhere to be seen. But Laura's relief was mingled with a feeling of disappointment she wasn't altogether sure she understood.

"There you are, Laura." Mac greeted her with a smile. "Carly said you were taking a shower."

"Yes, I was," she replied.

"Tanner was up here looking for you," Mac continued.

"Oh!" Laura felt her heart lurch painfully.

"He wanted to tell you not to wait dinner for him. The marine supply shop called and those parts I ordered a couple of weeks ago came in. He's gone into town to pick them up and he said he'd probably grab a bite to eat while he's there," explained Mac.

"Fine." Laura was relieved that her reprieve had been extended for a while. "Come on, you two," she went on. "Time to set the tables in the dining room for me."

"What's for supper?" Craig asked, hopping down from the bed.

"Homemade meat pies and a green salad."

Carly followed her brother and it was on the tip of Laura's tongue to ask her daughter if she'd mentioned the picnic to Tanner, but she stifled the impulse, feeling sure that in time Carly would readily volunteer the information.

As Laura turned to follow the twins, Mac spoke. "How long do you think he'll stay?" he asked. The question brought Laura to a halt and she turned to Mac, unsure whether or not she'd heard a wistful note in his voice.

"Perhaps you should ask Tanner that question," she said softly, crossing to the bed.

"I... Well..." Mac floundered, dropping his gaze to his hands, and Laura noted the pink tint of embarrassment on his cheeks. "I just thought he might have said something to you," he hurried on.

"No, he hasn't." She sat on the edge of the bed. "But I did get the impression he's here to mend a few fences," she continued, reaching out to touch his hands.

Mac glanced up at her. "What fences?" he asked, his tone instantly defensive, obviously thinking she was referring to a fence somewhere on the property.

Laura shook her head and smiled. "The fences I'm talking about are the invisible ones you and Tanner have built between you over the years."

This time Mac did meet her gaze and she glimpsed an emotion she couldn't define in the depths of his eyes. "I suppose I should be grateful he showed up when he did," Mac said gruffly, and Laura was pleased that there was no rancor in his tone.

"That's a start," Laura said, bending forward to kiss his leathery cheek. "Tanner is, and always will be, your son, Mac."

Again something flickered in Mac's eyes at the gentle reminder and his expression grew thoughtful, but he said nothing. Laura rose from the bed and headed downstairs.

Later, while supervising the twins' bath time, her thoughts returned to those moments in Mac's bedroom. Tanner's arrival had obviously affected Mac more than he was willing to admit. Laura found herself wondering if perhaps the time Mac had spent with the twins during the past month had brought back memories of happier days when Tanner and Billy were children.

"Are we going to call Grandma, now?" Craig asked, breaking into her thoughts.

"As soon as the two of you are in your jammies."

"It's my turn to push the numbers," Carly said, as Laura helped her daughter with her pajama top.

"No, it's mine," Craig retorted, as he struggled to put his on over a body that hadn't been properly dried.

"If you're going to argue," Laura cautioned, "neither of you will push the numbers." At this the twins glared at each other.

Downstairs in the living room Craig relented and let his sister do the honors.

After an exchange of greetings Carly immediately started talking about Tanner. Minutes later Carly dutifully handed the telephone to her brother who proceeded to tell his grandmother about Mac's mishap as well as to give her an account of the unsuccessful fishing trip he and his sister had taken with Tanner.

While the children took turns talking to Irene, Laura went to the kitchen to set out their bedtime treat of a glass of milk and some cookies.

"Grandma wants to talk to you now," Craig said when she returned a few minutes later.

Laura took the receiver and held her hand over the mouthpiece. "Milk and cookies are on the kitchen table and when you're finished, run upstairs. If you ask Mac politely, maybe he'll read you a bedtime story."

The twins scurried off and Laura took a deep breath knowing full well her mother would be itching with curiosity and undoubtedly would have a list of questions—all of them about Tanner.

"Hello, Mother."

"Laura? Darling? Is everything all right?" Irene asked, more than a hint of anxiety in her voice. "The twins were rambling on about Tanner, but I wasn't exactly sure... I mean, they're not talking about their fath—" she broke off. "They can't mean *Tanner*—not Mac's son?"

"Yes, actually they do," Laura said on a sigh.

Her mother gasped. "But, Laura. Good heavens. You mean he's there? At Moonbeam Lake? But I thought you said he hadn't seen his father for years. When did he arrive? He doesn't know about the twins, does he? You haven't told him? What *are* you going to do?"

"Calm down, Mother," Laura said, as a headache started to throb at her temples. "Yes, it is Tanner—" she glanced around to make sure no one was in earshot "—and no, he doesn't know about the twins."

"How long is he staying?" Irene asked.

"I don't know," Laura replied, thinking that was a question everyone seemed to want to know the answer to, including her.

"The way the children talked about him, they certainly seem to have taken a shine to him," Irene commented.

"Yes, they have." Laura still wasn't sure what she thought about that.

"Has he asked you any questions...? I mean... You know..." Irene came to a halt.

"He knows I don't have a husband. But how he interprets that is anyone's guess."

"What if he should ask you about the twins' father? What will you tell him?"

Apprehension shimmied through Laura but she quickly controlled it. "I'll cross that bridge when I come to it," she responded, managing to keep any hint of concern from her voice.

Suddenly she heard the sound of tires on the gravel outside and the anxiety she'd been trying to hold at bay descended on her once more.

"Mother, I have to go. It's time the twins were in bed. Oh, by the way, they want to know when you can come for a visit."

"I'm dying to, of course," came the eager reply. "Especially now. Maybe I should just close the restaurant for a few days." She paused for a moment. "I can't promise, but tell the children I'll see what I can do," she concluded.

"I'll tell them," Laura said. "Talk to you soon, Mother." As Laura replaced the receiver she suddenly realized that she hadn't asked her mother how things were going at the restaurant.

Up until a month ago the restaurant had been a major priority in her life, as well as a major source of stress. But since coming to work in the relative peace and tranquillity of Moonbeam Lake, the level of stress had diminished considerably. The atmosphere here was far more relaxed and, Laura silently admitted to herself, her working environment held few of the pressures she'd once encountered on a daily basis.

The sound of a car door closing jolted her from her reverie, spurring her into action. She was sure it was Tanner returning and she hurried from the room hoping to make it up the stairs before he reached the porch.

She wasn't quite quick enough. As she crossed to the stairs, Tanner, carrying a brightly colored bag in his hand, appeared in the doorway.

Her pulse skittered to a halt at the sight of him, before gathering speed once more. It wasn't fair, she thought with growing dismay as he flashed her a smile, that his smile could create such havoc within her.

"Are the twins in bed?" he asked.

"Not quite," she replied, meeting his gaze and feeling the jolt of awareness that was becoming all too familiar.

"Good. Because I brought them each a present."

"A present?" Laura repeated, surprised and strangely moved by the excitement she could hear in his voice.

"It's not much," he went on a hint of shyness creeping into his tone. "I picked up a couple of yo-yos," he explained, holding up the bag in his hand. "You don't mind do you? I just thought they'd get a kick out of them."

"Of course I don't mind," she said, knowing how much the twins loved getting presents. "It's very kind of you."

"Forget it. Every kid should have one." He cut off her attempt to thank him. "They were a source of countless hours of fun for Billy and me when we were kids. We both got to be pretty proficient with them, but Mac had us beat," he added, a smile of reminiscence on his face.

"Really?" Laura was again finding it difficult to resist the pull of his smile.

"Even though he's in bed, I wouldn't be surprised if he could still show us a few moves," Tanner bragged. "Why don't we find out?" he asked.

"I'll believe it when I see it," said Laura, caught up in Tanner's enthusiasm.

Carly and Craig were thrilled with their presents and it wasn't long before Mac's bedroom was filled with the sound of laughter.

In the midst of the fun and excitement Tanner went to his room and returned with one of his cameras. He began to snap pictures at random, all the while thinking that he couldn't recall a time when he'd had as much fun.

He focused on Craig, frowning in concentration as he rewound the string on his toy, before turning to Carly who was standing at the foot of Mac's bed. He snapped several shots of her grinning up at him as she sent the yo-yo spinning.

Tanner marveled at how quickly the twins had captured his heart and as his gaze lingered on Carly, he again found himself wondering why she seemed familiar, and just who it was she reminded him of.

"All right, you two. It's time to brush your teeth and get into bed." Laura's voice cut through his musings and he turned to look at her standing in the doorway.

Their glances collided for a moment and he saw an emotion dance briefly in her gray-green eyes before she looked away. Fascinated, he watched as a blush spread over her face, accentuating the delicate features and emphasising the creamy texture of her skin.

He knew instinctively that she was recalling that electrifying moment when he'd glimpsed her standing naked in the bathroom. Fleeting though the moment had been, he'd been caught off guard by the sudden quickening of his pulse and the sharp but unmistakable tug of desire.

Not for the first time since his arrival, Tanner found his thoughts turning to the man who'd chosen to walk away from Laura and the twins. She'd said she had no husband and Tanner was slowly becoming convinced that whoever he was, the man had to have been a world-class fool.

"Can't we stay up a little longer?" Craig asked, a pleading note in his voice.

Not without some difficulty, Tanner dragged his attention back to the child. "You can practice with your yo-yo all day tomorrow, and the next day."

"I'm gonna sleep with mine under my pillow," Carly said, as she jumped down from the bed.

"Me, too," Craig said, trying unsuccessfully to stifle a yawn.

"Thank Tanner again for the gifts and then say good-night, please," Laura instructed in a tone that brooked no further resistance.

"Thank you, Tanner," Craig said.

"Thank you, Tanner," echoed Carly.

"'Night!"

"'Night, Tanner! 'Night, Mac!" They chorused before following their mother from the room.

Tanner turned to his father. "Great kids, aren't they?"

"You can say that again," Mac said, his tone warm.

"Has Laura ever mentioned their father to you?" Tanner asked.

"No," Mac replied coolly. "Why?" he asked abruptly.

"Just curious," Tanner said, hearing the hint of censure in his father's voice.

"Did you get the parts for that motor?" Mac changed the subject.

"Yes. Which reminds me, I left them out in the car. I'd better bring them in," he said.

"And you'd better check the boats, make sure they're tied up properly."

"I'll take care of it." Tanner kept his tone even.

"See that you do," Mac said.

Tanner bit back the angry retort that sprang to his lips, as well as the feelings of frustration that accompanied it.

Although the hostility he'd met with on his arrival had definitely dissipated, he was beginning to wonder if Mac was only being more sociable because he needed help until he was on his feet again.

For the remainder of the week the days fell into something of a pattern. Laura became adept at avoiding being alone with Tanner, and much to her relief the picnic she'd suggested had to be postponed because of inclement weather.

Tanner in turn was kept busy as the campsites unexpectedly filled up when a group of six retired couples from Florida, traveling together in a convoy of campers, decided to spend a few days at the resort. He had to restock the bait, cut more wood and attend to some minor boat repairs.

Mac's knee was slower to heal than he'd anticipated and by the time Friday rolled around he was bored and frustrated.

On a trip into town to pick up more parts for the motor, Tanner rented a pair of crutches and Mac was grudgingly grateful to be able to leave his room.

Mac spent most of Friday sitting on the old rocking chair on the porch, chatting to everyone who came to see how he was, as well as keeping a watchful eye on the children.

Tanner, who was working nearby trying to repair a boat motor, was subjected to suggestions and advice from his father. As she passed by, Laura marveled at the way Tanner remained unruffled throughout.

Every chance they got, the twins dogged Tanner's footsteps, but he didn't seem to mind. Like his father, he treated the children with patience and kindness as well as a sense of fun.

Though concerned at Carly and Craig's growing fondness for Tanner, Laura was at a loss to know how to curtail the time they spent with him, sure that any comment or action on her part would result in hurt feelings and questions from both the children and Tanner.

Saturday morning dawned bringing an influx of scheduled arrivals. As Saturday was always a busy day, Laura spent the morning preparing food for the pot-luck supper and dance held at the resort every Saturday evening during the summer season.

The supper and dance were held in the dining room and, weather permitting, the large set of sliding doors leading out to the porch were usually left open, allowing people to eat on the picnic tables outside if they wished to or to sit and watch the dancing in the dining room.

The day had been hot and sticky and while the twins were helping Tanner move the stereo and speakers into the dining room for the dance, Laura had taken the opportunity to indulge in a refreshing shower. The evening promised to be warm and sultry and in an attempt to stay cool, Laura opted to wear a floral summer dress with spaghetti straps.

Pinning her hair to one side with a tortoiseshell comb she studied her reflection for a long moment, trying to ignore the pinpricks of excitement and anticipation dancing across her skin. The supper and dance was just a friendly get-together put on for the campers and their families staying at the resort; it gave them a chance to get to know each other or to get reacquainted. Since she and the twins had arrived at Moonbeam Lake they'd taken part in similar gatherings. So why did she feel as if an army of butterflies had suddenly decided to camp out in her stomach?

Laura silently insisted that her excitement had nothing to do with the fact that Tanner would be there. But as she hurried downstairs to put the finishing touches to the smorgasbord, she couldn't quite control the jittery feelings she was experiencing.

As people started to arrive Laura handed out plates and told everyone to help themselves. She ate while keeping an eye on everyone. Children of varying ages, ranging from babies to teenagers, mixed and mingled and the adults were soon chatting with new or old friends.

Laura delivered a plate of food to Mac who was sitting at a picnic table outside talking to several of the retired couples. The twins were sitting at a table with a group of children, and Laura spotted Tanner in the dining room speaking with the two families who were renting cabins one and two.

He, too, had taken time out to shower and change, she noted, and was dressed in a pair of tan slacks and a pale green short-sleeved shirt that enhanced the rich dark tan on his arms and neck.

She noticed, too, that several of the women were casting admiring glances at Tanner but he seemed oblivious to the attention, deep in discussion with one of the men.

As was the custom, everyone helped to clear away the dishes and push aside the tables in readiness for the dance. Laura, along with Grace and John, and Kathy and Floyd—two of the retired couples traveling together—worked as an efficient team to wash and dry the dishes in record time.

Several couples and some young children were already dancing when Laura shooed her helpers out of the kitchen, assuring them she'd join them in a matter of minutes.

She found the twins with a small group of children sitting at a picnic table outside, listening intently to Mac telling stories about his fishing exploits. Laura didn't intrude, but simply stood watching in the doorway enjoying the cool evening air drifting up from the lake.

She turned to watch the couples dancing and as the music changed to a slow romantic ballad she couldn't help noticing one young couple who'd instantly jumped to their feet smiling at each other with love and laughter in their eyes.

Laura couldn't take her eyes off them as the young man drew the woman into his arms, bringing her body close to his. That they were very much in love was patently obvious and watching them Laura felt the sting of tears at the sight of such happiness.

Six years ago she'd had to make a hard choice. She'd had to face up to reality and forget her dreams of love and happily-ever-afters. Harsh though that reality had been, she'd accepted her fate, but always at the back of her mind she'd felt cheated.

An incurable romantic, she still harbored fantasies of one day being wooed and won over by the man of her dreams.

All through high school she'd never had a boy-friend; had never experienced the full spectrum of emotions that went hand in hand when two people were strongly attracted to each other. Not for her a declaration of love or a romantic proposal.

But she had no regrets. Not when she'd been blessed with two such beautiful and loving children. The twins had taken up all her energy and she'd been too busy caring and providing for them to take time out for herself and her own emotional needs.

Laura smiled wistfully at the couple still circling the floor, wrapped in each other's arms, oblivious of the people around them.

Suddenly a figure stepped in front of her blocking her vision and instantly her heart did a cartwheel as she recognized Tanner.

Before she knew what was happening, he took her hand in his and pulled her onto the dance floor and into his arms. Emotions and sensations she'd thought were dead and buried exploded to life within her, filling her with dizzying excitement.

Her initial instinct was to push him away, to free herself from his arms, but when she brought her hand to his chest her fingers disobeyed her brain's urgent command and slid across his chest and up around his neck.

The fact that she'd been watching the young couple and thinking about love and romance was undoubtedly the reason she found him too hard to resist.

With a sigh she closed her eyes and gave herself up to the wonder of being in his arms again, drinking in the earthy male scent that was the essence of this man, while the memory of another night, another time danced inside her head.

Tanner wasn't quite sure what had prompted him to pull Laura onto the dance floor. His intention had been to get some fresh air but when he'd seen her standing at the doorway with a dreamy look in her eyes, he'd simply acted on impulse.

Beneath his fingers her skin felt like silk and the perfume she wore teased his nostrils, reminding him of sweet spring flowers and hot summer rain. She fit against him as though they were two halves of a whole and as they moved together to the seductive rhythm of the music he felt his blood stir in his veins and a need he hadn't felt in a long time began to claw at his insides.

There was something achingly familiar about the way she felt in his arms, almost as though he'd held her like this before. But he couldn't recall ever dancing with Laura... His thoughts careened to a halt. But he had held Leanne in his arms. Was that it? he wondered. Was he simply confusing Laura with her cousin?

That had to be the explanation. And yet...

Laura was drifting on a sea of sensation, riding on a moonbeam, wishing the music would never stop.

During the past six years she'd locked away the memories of the night Tanner had made love to her, when he'd awakened the sensual woman deep within. Those memories had been all she'd had to sustain her through some dark and pain-filled moments.

Being in Tanner's arms again was as tormenting as it was pleasurable and Laura knew she'd be foolish to allow herself to even begin to hope or dream.

Hadn't she discovered firsthand that dreams were nothing more than illusions, illusions that disappeared in the harsh light of day?

Chapter Seven

The last notes of the seductive love song slowly faded away but before Laura or Tanner could move apart, the rousing sound of a polka filled the room. In a matter of seconds, everyone, including the children who'd been sitting outside on the deck, was on the dance floor, either clapping their hands or dancing.

Tanner swung Laura around and around, their steps marking perfect time with the music. Amid laughter and loud cries they were jostled and bumped on the crowded floor, and when they came around for the second time to the doorway leading outside, Tanner deftly maneuvered her onto the deserted deck.

With their arms still around each other they came to a halt, both trying with difficulty to catch their breaths. Laughing now, Laura drew an arm's length away from Tanner and looked up at him.

As their glances collided, the air between them was suddenly alive with tension, and Laura felt excitement surge through her as she watched Tanner's eyes darken to a midnight blue.

He held her gaze for the space of a heartbeat, just long enough for the sparks arcing between them to ignite a need she'd only ever felt once before in her life.

His head dipped toward her in a slow tantalizing motion, sending a dizzying heat spiraling through her. But as his lips brushed her own in a feather-light caress, a feeling of panic suddenly swooped down like an icy northerly wind, effectively dousing the flames of desire and sending a cold shiver through her.

"No!" The denial burst from her lips as she broke the contact, and Laura's blood thundered in her ears as she watched the expression in the depths of his eyes change, first to surprise, then to puzzlement.

Seizing her chance, Laura stepped out of the circle of his arms and a feeling of relief washed over her when he made no move to impede her.

"I'm sorry," Tanner said, dropping his hands to his side.

Laura struggled to find something to say to fill the awkward, embarrassing silence that stretched between them. "I ... It's just that ..." she began.

"No problem," Tanner quickly cut in. "I was out of line..." He ran a hand through his hair in a gesture that shouted frustration.

Behind them the last strains of the polka were dying away and the dancers and spectators were applauding, totally unaware of the drama being played outside.

"I think I'll round up the twins. It's time they went to bed," Laura said, wanting only to escape and to avoid having to make small talk with the people beginning to spill out onto the deck.

Tanner made no reply and Laura turned and wound her way through the dancers as a waltz began to play. She glanced around the room, quickly spotting the children near the kitchen door. Carly was sitting on her grandfather's lap, her head resting on his chest, gamely fighting to stay awake.

Craig stood next to Mac's chair, a wide grin on his face as he listened to something Mac was saying. At the look of happiness on Mac's face, Laura felt tears stinging her eyes and she found herself struggling with another set of emotions that added to the turmoil Tanner had unknowingly aroused within her.

As she gazed at the threesome in the corner she silently acknowledged that her decision to come to Moonbeam Lake had been the right one.

What she hadn't expected or anticipated was how quickly the twins had come to love Mac and he them. A fact that served only to compound her feelings of guilt and regret for having stayed away so long.

"Mom! Mac says his knee is feeling better and we might be able to go fishing tomorrow," Craig said as he caught sight of Laura and ran toward her.

Laura swallowed the lump in her throat and playfully ruffled her son's dark hair. "That's great," she managed to say. "Listen, I think it's time you and your sister were in bed."

"But it isn't ten o'clock yet," Craig protested.

"It's past ten, sweetheart. It's ten-thirty," she pointed out gently. "Your sister is nearly asleep already," she added, reaching forward to lift Carly into her arms.

"But, Mom . . ." Craig muttered.

"If there's no argument, we might have time to read a story," she told him, as Carly snuggled against her shoulder.

"Peter and the Wolf?" he asked, smiling up at her now.

"Sure," she replied.

"'Night, kids," Mac said.

With Craig leading the way, Laura headed for the stairs. Carly, asleep in her arms, was a deadweight and Laura was having trouble holding on to her. She stopped at the foot of the stairs and tried to get a better grasp of the sleeping child.

"Here, let me," Tanner said, and before she could argue he gently lifted Carly from her arms as though she were nothing more than a featherweight.

Laura reluctantly followed Tanner up the stairs, hoping that once he'd deposited Carly on her bed he would leave. But it was not to be. After carefully lowering Carly onto her bed Tanner turned to Craig. "Okay, sport. Where are your jammies?" he asked softly.

Laura hesitated in the doorway but only for a moment. After her encounter with Tanner downstairs, she was feeling emotionally drained and a little fragile—and being in such proximity to him was playing havoc with her senses. The emotions and sensations Tanner had aroused were still too close to the surface and she was increasingly afraid that he might tune in to the anxiety she was feeling and not only wonder at its cause, but question her.

Not without difficulty Laura concentrated on undressing Carly and putting a nightie on the sleeping child, but she was all too aware of Tanner behind her, on Craig's bed.

Try as she might to ignore the whispers and suppressed laughter coming from her son and the man who was his father, Laura suddenly found herself thinking that if anyone should happen to peek into the room, they would instantly assume that she and Tanner were a husband and wife putting their children to bed.

Laura's eyes immediately filled with tears at this thought. She blinked them away, glad that Carly was asleep and unable to comment on them as she surely would have done. She kissed her daughter's cheek and as she stood up she brushed accidentally against Tanner—an action that served to rekindle the emotions she was trying hard to repress.

"Aren't you going to read 'Peter and the Wolf' to me?" Craig asked, glancing up at his mother.

"It's late..." Laura ventured, anxious to leave.

"But, you said..." Craig began, his lower lip beginning to quiver.

"I'll read to you," Tanner offered. "Your mother's had a busy day. What say we give her the rest of the night off?" he suggested in a lighthearted tone.

"Okay," Craig said, before reaching for the book on the table between the beds. "Good night, Mom. I love you."

Moved by her son's words, it was all she could do to smile, and it took every ounce of her control to respond. "I love you, too." Her voice was husky with emotion.

Normally she would have kissed Craig good-night, but that would have resulted in bringing her close to Tanner once more, a situation she was determined to avoid.

"Good night," she added, and with a nod in Tanner's direction she made her escape.

Laura headed for the sanctuary of her bedroom and closing the door behind her she leaned heavily against it. During the past hour her emotions had been on a

roller coaster ride. She needed a few minutes to herself; time to regroup before rejoining the folks downstairs.

Tanner had been home less than a week and his presence was affecting her strongly and in ways she'd never
expected. Dancing with him, feeling his body close to
hers had aroused a need she'd never thought she'd feel
again. And when his mouth had brushed hers, the
fleeting touch had been enough to send her emotions
into riotous disorder.

But that deep inner instinct known as self-
preservation had also been awakened, warning her that
when Tanner kissed her, really kissed her, he might well
realize the truth—and discover that *she* and not her
cousin Leanne was the woman he'd made love to that
night six years ago.

Though the longing to taste again the bittersweet fla-
vor of his desire had been strong, the fear that his desire would turn to disbelief and then hate, had been far
more powerful. Not only had she deceived him, she had
deprived him of the knowledge that he had fathered
twins, and robbed him of some of the most important
years of their lives.

The blame lay solely with her and she accepted that
responsibility, but with each passing day the burden of
it was becoming harder and harder to bear.

The sound of footsteps in the hallway broke into her
reverie and Laura held her breath for a moment until
they faded. Much as she wanted to stay in her room and
avoid another meeting with Tanner, she couldn't simply abandon the guests.

Downstairs the gathering was beginning to thin out
and Laura was relieved when she glimpsed Tanner

heading toward the jetty, no doubt to make sure all the boats had been secured properly.

With the help of the few remaining guests, Laura quickly tidied up the dining room, and after thanking her helpers she wished them good-night.

Peeking in on the twins, Laura kissed them both and stood staring down at her children wondering, not for the first time, if she'd done the right thing when she'd made the decision not to contact Tanner when she'd found out she was pregnant.

At the time it had seemed her only option and the fact that they'd turned out so well without a father figure said a lot for the time and love and commitment she and her mother had given to the twins.

But Laura had to admit that after seeing them with Mac and Tanner, watching how they interacted and responded to a male influence, they'd already benefited from the contact. Having a man like Mac for a grandfather had enhanced and enriched the children's lives, and in the brief time since Tanner's arrival, he, too, had won over their hearts by showing a loving, caring side she hadn't known he possessed.

The guilt she felt was both real and painful, but much as she might want to appease her own conscience, she wasn't sure she was ready to pay the price. Besides, Tanner had returned to Moonbeam Lake to make peace with his father and though the progress he was making was slow, Laura felt confident that a reconciliation would happen.

And when the summer was over, Tanner would undoubtedly resume his career, a career that would take him to some far-off corner of the world.

Laura spent another restless night. Images of Tanner danced in her head and the pillow she clung to in an attempt to appease the ache was a poor substitute. She woke with a start and sat up in bed. Glancing at the clock on the bedside table she groaned aloud when she realized she'd slept in.

Pulling on shorts and a T-shirt she ran a brush through her hair and hurried to the twins' room. The beds were empty and Laura stood for a moment, surprised that the children hadn't come in to her room to wake her.

Frowning, she tried not to be too concerned, sure that Craig and Carly were with Mac and Tanner. Mac's room was also empty and Laura hurried downstairs to the kitchen.

The aromatic smell of coffee tantalized her as she reached the foot of the stairs. The twins were sitting quietly at a table eating cereal, and Tanner, wearing denim shorts and a white T-shirt, stood with his back to her at the stove.

In a reaction that was becoming all too familiar, she felt a rush of excitement at the sight of him.

"Hi, Mom!" Craig greeted her through a mouthful of cereal.

Laura swallowed convulsively. "Why didn't you two wake me?" she asked, relieved that her voice betrayed none of what she was feeling.

"'Cause Tanner told us not to." Carly supplied the answer.

"Good morning, Laura," Tanner said, turning from the stove, a mug of coffee in his hand, to flash her a smile. "I heard you tossing and turning last night, so I didn't think you'd mind being left to sleep a little later."

"Oh..." was all Laura could manage to say as she dropped her gaze, hoping he wouldn't notice the flush of heat that swept up her neck and into her cheeks.

Tanner watched in surprise as Laura's cheeks turned a delicate shade of pink. He hadn't intended to embarrass her, and her reaction puzzled him. The only reason he'd known she'd had a restless night was that he hadn't been able to get to sleep, either.

He'd been thinking of her. Thinking back to those moments on the porch when he'd held her in his arms and brushed his mouth over hers.

Though the touch had been fleeting, he'd been unprepared for the sharp tug at his senses, or the sudden quickening of his pulse. But what baffled him most was the overwhelming sense of déjà vu that had enveloped him during those unforgettable seconds.

When she'd abruptly pulled herself free of his arms, he'd felt strangely bereft, as though he'd lost something precious, and he'd lain awake for a long time, puzzled by the emotions Laura ignited within him whenever she was near.

"Aren't you two finished eating breakfast yet?" The question from Mac as he entered the room, cut through the silence.

"I am! I am!" Carly quickly assured him, pushing her plate aside.

"Me, too," Craig joined in.

"If we want to catch any fish today, we'll have to get cracking," Mac said, his tone teasing.

"Wanna come fishing with us, Tanner?" Carly asked, her deep blue eyes staring innocently up at him.

Laura held her breath, wondering if she should intervene, unsure of just how Mac would react.

Tanner threw his father a glance, expecting to see a look of anger or resentment at having been placed in such an awkward position, but there was no sign of either emotion in the depths of Mac's eyes.

"I hate to turn down a chance to go fishing," Tanner said carefully. "But I'm not sure..." His voice trailed off. The twins turned to Mac, their expressions eager.

"Well... I suppose there's enough room in the boat for one more..." Mac said with a guarded glance at his son.

"Then count me in," Tanner said, scarcely able to believe what he'd heard.

"Yeah!" the children chorused and Tanner couldn't stop the smile that curled at his mouth at their response.

The fact that his father had issued an invitation of sorts was, as far as Tanner was concerned, a major breakthrough. He couldn't remember the last time he and his father had gone fishing together, and he had two precocious five-year-olds to thank for giving him this chance.

"Let's get this show on the road," Mac said, turning to leave and immediately the children scurried to catch up with him.

After Mac, Tanner and the twins had left, Laura poured herself a mug of coffee and sat outside on the porch enjoying the morning sunshine. Though she often spent part of her time planning menus for the upcoming week and doing other small chores, she considered Sunday her day off.

Laura had been sorely tempted to invite herself along on the fishing expedition. She was used to spending Sunday with the children, but it had been obvious that they were much too excited about going fishing with Tanner and Mac to think of including her.

She tried to tell herself that she wasn't in the least upset that they hadn't asked her along, but as the morning passed into afternoon and she'd taken care of making beds and doing laundry for herself and the twins, she couldn't seem to concentrate on anything.

Feeling lonely and more than a little sorry for herself, Laura sat on the porch watching for the boat to return. Though the day was warm, white fluffy clouds floated by to block the sun.

Until coming to Moonbeam Lake, she'd been the one the children had always turned to whenever they were restless or bored or in need of some love and attention. She realized with a pang that she'd grown used to their dependency. But since coming here, their lives had expanded to include other people as well as new interests, an adjustment she wasn't sure she was ready to make.

Laura was in the kitchen making up a grocery list for the week ahead when she heard the children's excited voices outside. Tossing the pencil and paper aside, Laura hurried out to the porch to greet them.

"Look what Craig and me caught," Carly said, blue eyes glinting with pleasure and excitement as she ran toward her holding up two good-sized trout.

Craig, sporting a smile as wide as the lake itself, also held up two trout, one in each hand. "We caught them all by ourselves," he told her proudly.

Behind them, Mac and Tanner's faces were wreathed in smiles and Laura felt a warm glow wash over her as she saw a look of warmth and humor pass between Tanner and his father.

"Wow! That's terrific!" Laura said sincerely. "I'm very proud of you both."

"Tanner caught one, too, and so did Mac," Craig told her as he held out his prize.

"But bro and me caught the mostest," his sister was quick to point out. "Tanner says we can cook them for supper."

Laura smiled at her daughter. "I think that's a great idea. Any volunteers to clean them?" she asked hopefully, glancing up at the men.

"Whoever catches them has to clean them," Tanner said. "That's the rule, isn't it, Dad?" He turned to wink conspiratorially at Mac.

Laura saw the flash of emotion in Mac's eyes at Tanner's wink.

"Oh... Absolutely," Mac said, having difficulty keeping a straight face.

Carly was studying the fish in her right hand, her nose wrinkling in a look of distaste at the prospect of cleaning it. "I'm not hungry," she announced.

The sound of Tanner's deep rich laugh filled the air and a shiver of awareness chased through Laura leaving a strange longing in its wake.

Mac's laughter quickly followed and before long the children joined in, too, though they weren't altogether sure what they were laughing about.

"I'll clean them," Tanner said after a few moments. "But first I think we should get a photograph of you two with your catch. What do you say?"

"Yeah!" the children chorused.

"Run upstairs to my room, Craig, and bring me the camera that's sitting on the table by the bed."

Craig hurried off to do as he was told and when he returned, Tanner had the children pose on their own and then with Mac while he snapped the remainder of his film.

"Who wants to help me clean the fish?" he asked after rewinding the film and setting the camera aside.

"I will," Craig said, and at this Carly quickly thrust her catch at her brother.

As Mac, Tanner and Craig headed off to the sink and counter at the end of the lodge, set up for the sole purpose of cleaning the fish that were caught, Carly followed Laura into the kitchen.

"Can we bake cookies?" Carly asked, and with a nod Laura agreed. Fifteen minutes later when Carly was putting the first batch of cookies into the oven, her brother appeared in the doorway carrying the freshly cleaned fish in an ice-cream bucket.

"Tanner and Mac are going to work on the boat engine, now," Craig informed his mother. "Can I help with the cookies, too?" He eyed the cookie batter in the big bowl on the table hungrily.

"Wash your hands first," Laura instructed.

"Here," Carly said, handing her brother a spoon after he'd finished drying his hands.

Laura stood at the sink and smiled to herself as she watched the two of them work happily together.

The meal that evening was delicious. Laura had dipped the trout in a mixture of egg and milk and seasonings, then coated them with oatmeal and herbs before popping them into the hot skillet. Caesar salad, steamed vegetables and brown rice completed the dish and both Mac and Tanner complimented her several times on the meal.

They lingered over coffee and the twins proudly offered the chocolate chip cookies they'd made.

"Did you catch all the fish in the same spot?" Laura asked as she moved away from the sink where she'd put the dirty dishes to soak.

"Yes, we did. We were at the north end where that tiny creek the kids call the Mississippi flows into the lake. Craig caught the first one,'' Mac went on, and Craig nodded vigorously in confirmation.

"That's where the kids and I went the other day,'' Tanner said. "We were using worms, but we didn't have any luck.''

"What were you using today?'' Laura asked her son.

"A speckled green flatfish,'' Craig informed her.

"Mine was yellow,'' Carly said before taking another bite of her cookie.

"They both worked,'' Tanner said with a shake of his head. He was silent for a moment, then he smiled. "I remember Billy and I fishing in that same spot. We hadn't caught a darned thing all afternoon, though fish were jumping like crazy around the boat. We tried every lure we had in the tackle box, but nothing worked.

"Suddenly the clouds rolled in like they sometimes do around here, and it started to rain. And I do mean rain. We were soaked to the skin in seconds as we reeled in our lines. Billy reeled in his first and he started to row to shore when we heard this thud. I thought Billy had thrown something into the bottom of the boat and he said later he thought I had.

"We both looked around and there in the boat, flapping away like mad, was one of the biggest trout we'd ever seen.'' Tanner chuckled at the memory.

"Who caught it?'' Craig wanted to know.

Tanner shook his head. "Nobody. The silly thing had just jumped right into the boat all by itself. No one believed us, of course,'' he added, still smiling.

The children were laughing now and Laura glanced at Mac, wondering how he would react to Tanner's story about Billy, but to her relief and surprise he was smiling, too.

"Billy sure loved to fish," Mac said, his voice warm with love and remembrance. "Even when he was supposed to be doing his chores he'd have a line in the water somewhere. I remember one day when he was chopping wood down by the lakeshore. He'd set his rod up on one of the small rowboats he'd hauled up on shore.

"He was bobber fishing, and Billy said later that he'd been glancing up occasionally to check on the bobber, when suddenly it disappeared. But before he could make a move toward the pole, his rod was yanked into the water and the last he saw of it, it was heading down the lake."

"You mean he lost his rod and everything?" Carly asked.

Mac took a sip of coffee before answering. "Not exactly," he said. "You see, I'd been out fishing and was on my way back in when I noticed something floating in the water near the middle of the lake. When I got closer I recognized Billy's rod. I grabbed for it and started to reel it in."

"That was lucky," Craig said, his gaze intent on Mac's. "I guess the fish must have broke the line and got away."

"Not only was the line not broken," Mac said, his face creasing into a smile. "But the fish was still on the hook."

The children laughed and clapped their hands and Laura joined in.

Tanner immediately started in with another fishing story and for the next thirty minutes the two men traded memories, most of them involving Billy.

Though it had been six years since his death, Laura was sure that this was the first time Tanner and his father had talked about him, together, and in such a loving way.

Memories were all they had left and Laura knew that even after all the time that had passed, talking about Billy, remembering the good times they'd shared with him was a way of keeping his memory alive and of working through their own grief.

As they talked, Laura had quietly and unobtrusively crossed to the sink and begun washing the dishes. To her surprise Tanner grabbed a towel and began to dry. The feeling of family and harmony was very strong and Laura felt tears prick her eyes at the thought of having to leave, of having to return to Vancouver when summer was over.

Suddenly the sound of voices could be heard coming from the dining room. But before anyone could move, the kitchen door swung open and Laura's mother stood smiling at her from the doorway.

"Surprise!" Irene cried, but Laura saw the anxious look her mother threw her.

"Surprise! Surprise!" said the woman who swept past Irene into the kitchen.

Laura's heart dropped to her toes at the sight of her cousin Leanne. Dressed in a stunning green silk jumpsuit, her dark brown hair cropped stylishly short, she looked as if she'd just walked off the pages of a fashion magazine.

Chapter Eight

Laura glanced at Tanner in time to see his face light up like a neon sign when he recognized the newcomer.

Pain, sharp and intense, stabbed at Laura's heart as she watched his reaction. The fact that the children had jumped down from their seats at the table and were noisily greeting their grandmother gave Laura a few seconds to regain her composure.

"Leanne! It's good to see you." Laura pinned a smile on her face and gave her cousin a hug.

"It's good to see you, too," Leanne said. "I can't believe how much the twins have grown since I saw them last fall." She smiled at the twosome who were intent on hugging their grandmother.

Laura turned to her mother who had crouched down to kiss the twins. "Mom, you remember Mac and Tanner?"

"Indeed I do," Irene replied, smiling up at them. "It's lovely to see you both again."

"The pleasure is all ours, Irene," Mac responded sincerely, rising slowly to his feet and touching his forehead in a salute.

"Mrs. Matthews," Tanner acknowledged.

Irene nodded to Tanner as she lifted Carly into her arms.

"Mac...Tanner," Leanne said, her gaze shifting from one to the other. "It's so good to see you both. How long has it been?"

"Six years," Tanner answered promptly, and for a moment Laura wondered if he was going to add the exact number of days and hours. "You look great," he continued as he gave her a welcoming embrace.

As Laura watched the interchange she felt as if someone had suddenly punched her in the midsection. She drew in a sharp breath, struggling to keep her emotions under control.

"Thank you," said Leanne. "I didn't expect to see you here," she went on. "Do you still gallivant all over the world taking pictures?"

"Not this summer," Tanner said, his gaze intent on Leanne. "What brings you to Moonbeam Lake? Laura didn't tell us you were coming."

"That's because she didn't know," Leanne responded easily. "I have a reputation for showing up out of the blue. It's a bad habit. But a girlfriend of mine works in a travel agency in Honolulu and whenever there's a cheap flight to the mainland or when there's some special promotion, she lets me know. It doesn't happen very often, a couple of times a year, maybe. But when it does I take advantage of it. I close up my boutique and off I go."

"How long will you be staying?" Tanner asked, and at his question Laura felt the ache in her heart intensify.

"I'm not sure. Probably only a couple of days," Leanne told him. "I'm actually heading to Toronto to see my folks. They're house-sitting for some friends who are off on a world cruise, and I thought it would be fun to surprise them. But when Aunt Irene told me Laura and the twins were spending the summer here at the lake... I just couldn't resist taking a side trip. Dad still has the cabin, you know. We stopped there first and walked over. Boy, did seeing the old place bring back a few memories," she concluded and smiled up at Tanner.

"Your father still likes to come up and get a bit of fishing in when he can," Mac said. "He has someone from town keeping an eye on the place."

"So, Tanner. Tell me, how are things with you?" Leanne asked.

"Looking better every day," he replied, his mouth curling into a sexy smile.

Laura felt as if a hand had closed around her heart. If only Tanner would smile at *her* that way, she thought with a sigh. But as always, Leanne tended to overshadow any other female in the room.

Laura had never tried to compete with her cousin, and she had to admit that the tailored, lime-green jumpsuit Leanne wore was the perfect foil for her tanned features and short dark hair. She had a healthy yet exotic look that was very attractive to men, judging by the way Tanner kept his eyes on her.

Glancing at her mother, Laura noted the look of anxiety in the depth of her eyes, and with an effort she managed a smile.

"Well, you two," Laura said, addressing the twins. "I think you've had enough excitement for one day. It's time to get ready for bed." At her words the children groaned.

"But Grandma just got here," Carly protested.

"Your grandma's going to give me a hand. Isn't that right?" Laura said, staring pointedly at her mother.

"Of course," Irene replied. "I'll even volunteer to read you a story."

"I get to pick the story," Craig said.

"No, I do," Carly quickly put in.

"Why don't I read you each a story?" their grandmother suggested with a knowing smile.

"Okay," they chorused.

"What are we waiting for?" Irene lowered Carly to the floor and took the child's hand in hers.

"There's still half a pot of coffee on the stove. Help yourselves," Laura said before following her mother and the twins from the kitchen.

Not having seen their grandmother for over a month, the twins were chattering nonstop, telling Irene about their fishing trip and the fish they'd caught.

As she made her way up the stairs Laura tried to ignore the feeling of nervousness that came over her at leaving Leanne alone with Mac and Tanner. But aside from dragging Leanne out of the kitchen there wasn't much she could do.

Over the years her cousin's habit of dropping in unannounced had at times been both annoying and inconvenient, and this time was no exception.

Though her visits were generally brief, when she'd appeared last fall out of the blue, she'd stayed more than a week. She'd told Laura that she'd left her husband, Justin, and was filing for divorce. She'd been distraught about the breakup and Laura had tried to be sensitive and supportive, but Leanne had been too caught up in her own misery to realize that her presence was affecting everyone, especially the children.

Laura had been worn to a frazzle trying to be a good listener, trying to keep the twins out of her cousin's way and trying to run a restaurant.

Gathering from what Laura had just seen, it was apparent Leanne had worked through the trauma of her divorce and was doing just fine. Could it be that when Irene had told Leanne that Tanner was at Moonbeam Lake, she'd come to visit for reasons other than simply to see an old friend?

Tanner's pleasure at seeing Leanne again had been evident, and Laura experienced a fresh stab of jealousy at the memory of the way he'd greeted her cousin.

Whatever transpired, Laura silently acknowledged that there was little she could do but pray Leanne's stay would be a brief one and that the subject of Billy and the night of his death would not become a topic of conversation.

"Laura, you haven't heard a word I've said," Irene complained.

They were upstairs in the bathroom and Irene was helping Carly out of her clothes. Craig was already undressed, busy trying to tie the ends of a towel around his neck to form a cape.

"What? Oh... I'm sorry," Laura said, and immediately reached for the faucet. "What were you saying?"

"I was telling you about Leanne," her mother said.

"What about her?" Laura glanced at her mother, trying not to sound anxious.

"Whee!" Craig yelled, effectively drawing Laura's attention away from Irene. He lifted his arms to form wings and headed for the door.

"And just where do you think you're going, young man?" Laura grabbed her son before he could run past her.

"I was just going to show Tanner my cape." Craig's expression was serious.

"Not like that you're not," Laura said, trying not to smile. "In you go," she added as she pulled the towel over his head.

Carly quickly wriggled out of her grandmother's arms and climbed into the tub, sitting opposite her brother.

"What about Leanne?" Laura asked ten minutes later after she and her mother had finished helping the children into their pajamas.

"She's met someone," came the reply.

"Really?" Laura said, annoyed with herself at the feeling of relief she experienced hearing that piece of news.

"Yes, really. I heard all about him on the ferry trip over here," she went on. "His name is Carl Hutchins, he's forty-nine years old and he owns a chain of jewelry stores. He's rich and handsome and from what I've heard of him, just her cup of tea."

"That's wonderful," Laura said. "Come on you two, into bed."

"He's also in Toronto right now," Irene continued as she lifted her granddaughter onto the bed.

"How long are you staying, Grandma?" Craig asked as he climbed up beside Carly.

"Only until tomorrow afternoon, I'm afraid."

"Can't you stay longer?" Carly asked.

"I wish I could," Irene replied. "But I have to get back to the restaurant."

"Will you read me my story first? Please, Grandma?" Carly begged.

"I'll leave you to it," Laura said, picking the wet towels from the bed and bending to kiss the children good-night.

Towels in hand, Laura returned to the bathroom to clean up the puddles on the floor and put the room back in order. She deliberately lingered over the task, reluctant to return to the kitchen.

Regardless of the news that her mother had imparted about Leanne and a possible new love interest, Laura couldn't forget the way Tanner had looked at her cousin, nor could she forget the flash of speculation and interest she'd seen in his eyes.

With a sigh, Laura made her way to the kitchen. She still had the tables in the dining room to set for breakfast and she hadn't finished cleaning the pots and pans.

Hearing the sound of water running, she opened the kitchen door to find Mac alone at the sink, rinsing the last of the pots.

"Hey... that's what I get paid to do," Laura joked as she crossed toward him.

"And a good job you do, too," Mac said, setting the pot on the draining board.

"Where is everybody?" Laura asked, keeping her tone casual.

"Leanne said she was tired, something about jet lag. Tanner offered to walk her back to her family's cabin."

"Oh..." Laura said, aware once more of a sinking feeling in her midsection.

"Leanne hasn't changed much, has she?" Mac wrung out the dish cloth.

"I guess not," Laura replied.

"Lives in Hawaii, does she?"

"Yes," Laura said. "She met her husband there."

"He didn't come with her?"

"No, they're divorced," Laura explained.

"Divorce," Mac said with a sigh. "Seems to be a way of life these days." He shook his head. "You never met my wife, did you?"

"No, I didn't."

"Kathleen Mary Elizabeth McLeod...a beautiful name for a beautiful woman." Mac was silent for a long moment. "Kathleen and I were deeply in love and we stayed that way for fifteen wonderful years...the happiest years of my life," he said, his voice reverberating with both love and sadness. "She was a remarkable woman and I still miss her." The longing in his voice was clear.

"Kathleen wanted half a dozen babies," Mac went on, almost as if he were talking to himself. "But for a long time we wondered if we'd ever have any—then Tanner arrived. He was our pride and joy. How we loved him." Again he was silent. "It was another eight years before Billy came on the scene—we'd about given up hope.

"Two years later my lovely Kathleen was gone and my whole life was turned upside down." Mac's tone was threaded with anguish and sorrow. "Billy was so young and he needed me. Tanner did, too, but each time I looked at them they reminded me so much of Kathleen." He stopped and took a steadying breath. "If it hadn't been for Tanner... I never would have gotten through those dark days.

"Almost before I knew it, Tanner was eighteen and telling me he was leaving home, going to Toronto then

New York to pursue a career in photography. Oh...he had the talent and the drive, all right, but that didn't mean we weren't going to miss him. Billy took it hard but we hung in there. We had each other.

"The next thing I know Billy's telling me *he's* leaving, that he's bought a ticket to Europe and he's off to see the world. It was too much...." Mac's voice wavered and Laura instinctively put her hand on his and squeezed it.

She wished there was something she could say that would ease the pain she heard in his voice. She doubted he'd ever told anyone what he'd just told her and she felt humbled that Mac trusted her enough to share his feelings. For the first time, she understood how devastated he must have felt the night Billy told him he was leaving.

Being a mother herself, now, Laura knew how strong the bonds were between a parent and a child. She wasn't looking forward to the twins starting kindergarten in the fall, all too aware that it was the first step in learning to let go.

But she also knew she had to let them go, that she would have to accept that there would be new influences, new challenges, and it would be up to her to help the children make the transition into the next phase of their young lives.

Had Mac's wife, Kathleen, still been alive, she would undoubtedly have helped him cope with the fact that like Tanner, Billy wanted to pursue his dream—wanted to explore life on his own terms. But on hearing Billy's plans to leave, Mac had reacted in anger, deeply hurt that his youngest son was also leaving home. He just hadn't known how to deal with the pain.

"Mac...Billy loved you very much, you have to know that," she said softly.

Laura saw the tears in Mac's eyes as he turned to her. "But it was my fault..." he said, his voice choked with emotion. "If I hadn't lost my temper..."

"Mac, don't. The accident wasn't your fault. You have to stop blaming yourself," she chided gently. "Angry words were spoken that night, it's true. But you can't dwell on that, you have to remember all the happy times you had together—just like you were doing with Tanner tonight."

"I've been such a stubborn old fool...I blamed Tanner...I turned my back on him.... How can he ever forgive me?"

"He's here now," Laura pointed out. "And I have a feeling everything will work out between the two of you. You'll see," she assured him.

"Thanks, Laura," Mac said. "I think having you and the twins here these past weeks started me off thinking about the past—about a lot of things."

Warmed by his words, Laura was sorely tempted, for a brief moment, to tell Mac the truth about the twins. She was convinced he would welcome the news, but she hesitated, not sure she would be able to live with the consequences.

"Tanner's back," Mac's words cut into her thoughts. Glancing out of the kitchen window, Laura saw Tanner approaching and immediately she felt her senses heighten.

Tanner slowed his pace as he approached the lodge. He didn't mind admitting to himself that he was thoroughly confused. Leanne's unexpected arrival at the lake had appeared to him to be a stroke of fate.

He'd offered to walk her back to her father's cabin for the sole purpose of spending time alone with her. He'd hoped to bring the conversation around to that night six years ago and perhaps take the first steps toward renewing their friendship.

But throughout the journey along the lakeshore Leanne had done most of the talking, chatting continuously about herself; about the boutique she ran, about the house her lawyer had retained for her out of the divorce settlement and about the divorce itself.

He'd listened and commented from time to time but she'd hardly heard him, so intent on telling him what had been happening in her life.

When she'd invited him in for a nightcap he'd politely declined, and as he turned and headed back he'd felt somewhat relieved to be on his own once again.

What he found difficult to come to terms with was how much Leanne had changed. Somehow the memory of the warm, caring, giving woman who'd helped him through the worst nightmare of his life, was a far cry from the woman he'd just spent the last twenty minutes with.

While he was willing to accept the fact that over time the mind tended to romanticize certain memories, to enhance their importance or significance, he had to admit that Leanne seemed to be a different person entirely from the woman he remembered.

He felt both cheated and disappointed and silently berated himself for being such a romantic fool. For the past six years he'd treasured those memories, been haunted by a woman he hadn't been able to forget but who in reality had been forgettable indeed.

Tanner shook his head in an attempt to dispel the negative thoughts floating around him. Through the kitchen window he could see his father and Laura, and they appeared to be deep in conversation.

His thoughts switched to Laura and he found himself comparing her with her cousin. Since his arrival at the lake, Laura had impressed him as being a hardworking young woman whose family was of the utmost importance to her.

Tanner guessed that from the way she'd reacted to questions about the twins' father, the man had probably vamoosed when he'd learned she was pregnant.

He admired her courage and the fact that not only had she accepted the responsibility of caring for the children, she'd done an admirable job. Somehow he couldn't picture Leanne as a loving mother, nor could he imagine her being content to live in such an outlying area as Moonbeam Lake.

It was obvious that Laura cared about Mac, and he was almost sure that her presence, along with the twins', had had a positive effect on his father.

Tonight for the first time since Billy's death, they'd actually talked about Billy, shared stories and memories. But Tanner was convinced that having Laura and the twins around had mellowed his father somewhat. Otherwise Tanner doubted the conversation would ever have taken place.

"Tanner, you look like you're deep in thought," Irene said as she came down the stairs.

"I was," he admitted as the screen door closed behind him. "Are the children asleep?"

"Almost," Irene replied.

"You must miss them," he commented, realizing as he spoke that he'd miss the twins, too, when the time came for them to return to the mainland.

Irene nodded. "Very much." They entered the kitchen together.

Laura turned at the sound of her mother's voice and smiled a greeting—deliberately avoiding looking at Tanner, fearful of what she might see in his eyes.

"Leanne's left already, Mother," Laura said. "I'll walk you back to the cabin."

"Thank you, darling," Irene said. "I told the twins I'd come by in the morning but I want to make sure I catch the ferry at two."

"You're leaving tomorrow?" Mac questioned.

"I'm afraid so," Irene responded. "Much as I'd love to stay and spend time with the children, I have a restaurant to run."

"You have two wonderful grandchildren there." Mac's voice held a hint of envy.

Irene smiled. "I know," she said softly.

Laura hooked her hand through her mother's arm as they made their way to the lake and along the path that would take them to the cabin. They were both silent for several minutes and it was Irene who finally spoke.

"I think you should tell him."

Laura drew a steadying breath before answering. "It's not as easy as that," she said.

"Carly and Craig love Tanner already, and Mac, too, for that matter," Irene pointed out.

"I know...I know..." A lump of emotion formed in Laura's throat.

"Then why don't you just tell him?" her mother repeated.

"I can't," Laura said.

"Why not?"

"I'm scared, that's why." Laura hated herself for her weakness. "Did you see the expression on his face when he saw Leanne?" she continued, pain twisting at her insides at the memory. "I can't tell him...I just can't."

"I'm sorry, darling. I don't mean to upset you. Do you want to come in for a minute?" Irene asked when they reached the cabin.

"No...I'd better get back," Laura said. "Thanks for coming, Mom, the kids miss you...and I do, too."

"I'll see you in the morning." Her mother drew Laura into her arms.

Laura fought the urge to let the tears fall and even managed a smile as she kissed her mother's cheek. "Good night," she said.

Laura began to walk back to the lodge, but when she reached the path that would take her to the place where Tanner had made love to her, she turned in that direction.

Since arriving at the lodge she'd deliberately avoided this trail, but tonight her usual resolve seemed to have abandoned her and she simply followed her impulse.

A crescent moon and a zillion stars sent a muted light over the lake and surrounding area and as Laura rounded a row of bushes that bordered the path, a large gray cloud suddenly passed in front of the moon.

Laura slowed to a halt and stood in the hushed silence waiting for the cloud to pass. An owl hooted somewhere in the distance and Laura drew a deep breath drinking in the peace and tranquillity.

As the cloud drifted past and what little light there was returned, Laura began to move on. Suddenly a shadowy figure sitting on a rock came into view bringing her to an abrupt halt.

Tanner! Instinct and senses acutely attuned to his presence, sent the message to her brain and her heart lurched inside her breast, even as her pulse picked up speed.

Reluctant as she was to approach him, she would have to retrace her steps practically all the way back to the cabin in order to take the alternate route home.

Gazing at his silhouette and seeing that he appeared to be deep in thought, Laura hesitated, wondering if she might manage to slip by without disturbing him. But before she could make up her mind on which course to take, Tanner glanced in her direction and immediately stood up, leaving Laura no alternative but to walk toward him.

"I hope I didn't disturb you," she said as she drew abreast of him.

"No... you didn't," Tanner assured her. "I was just sitting here doing some thinking," he said.

"I'll leave you to it," she said, hoping he'd let her escape, but it was not to be.

"That's okay. I'll walk back with you," he said and fell into step beside her. "I noticed you and my father were having a deep discussion earlier."

"He was talking about your mother and you and Billy," Laura said after a moment's hesitation.

"He was?" Tanner said, surprise in his voice.

"He still misses her... your mother, I mean."

"He loved her very much," Tanner said softly.

"That's what he said," Laura acknowledged, bewildered by the ache that suddenly caught at her heart.

Tanner stopped abruptly and put his arm out to halt her. "You mean he told you how he felt about my mother?"

"Yes," Laura replied, trying to ignore the frisson of heat radiating from where his hand touched her.

"But he never talks about her. Did he say anything else?" he asked, his eyes intent on Laura now.

A shiver of awareness danced across her skin as she met his gaze. "Well . . . ah . . . he talked about how devastated he was after your mother died, and how in no time at all you told him you were leaving home to pursue a career in photography." She stopped, noting that Tanner was focused on a spot over her shoulder. She wasn't sure he was even listening to her.

"Go on," Tanner prompted, bringing his gaze back to hers.

"And then when Billy told him he was leaving, too, well, he said it was just too much . . ." Her voice trailed off.

"He really said all that?" Tanner's tone was still disbelieving.

"Yes," Laura said.

"Did you weave some kind of magic spell on him?" he asked, a faint smile curving at the corners of his mouth.

Laura felt her breath catch in response to the smile. "No . . . I think just talking about Billy at supper . . . and remembering happier times . . ." She came to a halt.

"I believe you deserve the thanks for that."

"Me? I don't understand," Laura said as her senses jumped into high gear at his words.

"You and the children," Tanner said as he began to walk on. "Mac seems to have mellowed, and I think it has something to do with having you and the twins around. He was a terrific father, you know. He went through a rough patch when my mother died, and for a while he was just lost without her."

"I know," Laura said softly, remembering the pain she'd heard in Mac's voice. "He also told me he regrets the way he treated you when Billy died."

Tanner slowed to a stop as they reached the driveway leading to the lodge and was silent for a long moment. "I wish he'd tell me that," he said at last.

Laura turned to face Tanner, fighting down the urge to touch him, to soothe away the look of pain and regret she could see on his face. "It's never easy for anyone to admit they were wrong. And as hours or days and sometimes years pass it becomes even more difficult." She had trouble keeping the emotion out of her voice.

"You sound as though you're talking from experience," Tanner said, and at his perceptive comment Laura quickly closed her eyes and turned away, fearful that he might see the guilt she was trying hard to hide from him.

She shivered, but not from the cold. "I'd better check on the children," she said, knowing full well her excuse was flimsy at best.

"Tell me something," Tanner said, stopping her before she could walk away. "Do the twins ever see their father?"

Chapter Nine

Laura's heart shuddered to a halt then thudded noisily against her breastbone. Several long seconds ticked away before she could speak. "Why do you ask?" she said, her voice little more than a harsh whisper.

"Curiosity, I suppose. Look, I'm sorry. It's none of my business. Forget I asked," he hurried on. "Oh...and thanks."

"For what?" she asked, breathing a silent sigh of relief.

"For telling me about my father," he said. "It gives me hope that things might work out after all."

"I'm sure they will. Good night," she added over her shoulder as she climbed the steps leading to the porch.

Tanner waited until Laura was safely inside before turning and heading toward the jetty. He'd noticed the way she'd tensed at his question about the twins' father and, not for the first time, he wondered at the reason behind it.

The twins themselves never spoke of their father and Tanner couldn't help thinking this was unusual. That and the fact that Carly seemed so familiar, and Craig, too, to a degree, suggested that he might know the man. But as yet he hadn't been able to jog his memory.

As he checked the boats, his thoughts turned to what Laura had told him about her conversation with his father. That Mac had talked about his wife was most unusual, but Tanner felt warmed and encouraged by the news.

His own memories of his mother were quite vivid. As a child he'd loved to watch her unpin her golden-brown hair from the knot she always wore on top of her head. She'd let it fall to her shoulders, then brush it with sweeping strokes till it shone like polished gold. Billy's hair had been the same color as his mother's, while Tanner had inherited his father's dark coloring.

Suddenly Tanner remembered the old photograph that had once held pride of place on the upright piano in the living room. The picture had been of his parents on their wedding day; Mac looking proud and handsome and a little uncomfortable, dressed in a dark suit, white shirt and sporting a black bow tie. His mother had been wearing a plain white wedding gown of a simple style, yet Tanner remembered thinking how beautiful she'd looked, her eyes full of love as she'd gazed at his father.

That photograph along with countless others, including the ones missing from Billy's room, had to be in the attic. Perhaps he should retrieve them from their hiding place, bring them out and display them once more.

No time like the present, Tanner thought as he finished checking the last of the boats. Picking up his pace, he headed toward the lodge.

The house was quiet, an indication that everyone had gone to bed. On the upper landing, Tanner wasn't surprised to discover that the door to the attic was locked. Reaching up, he ran his fingers along the top of the doorframe and smiled to himself when he located the key.

Unlocking the door, he returned the key to its hiding place and with his shoulder gave the door a gentle nudge. He smiled again as it opened under a minimum of pressure, and quietly closing it behind him, he slowly climbed the stairs to the spacious attic.

When he reached the top, he yanked on the string dangling from the ceiling and immediately the room was bathed in the muted glow from the forty-watt light bulb that hung from the ceiling.

The attic was hot and stuffy and dusty from neglect but Tanner didn't notice. He knew exactly where he'd find the boxes of photographs and it wasn't long before he was seated in the old wicker rocking chair his mother had once used, the boxes on the floor by his feet and a handful of pictures from the first box in his lap.

Switching on an old floor lamp, Tanner began to thumb through the numerous photographs. Time drifted by unnoticed and more than once his eyes filled with tears and his throat closed over with emotion as he was flooded by memories.

He smiled when he came across a number of photos he'd taken with the camera his parents had given him on his ninth birthday.

Picking up another handful from the second box, Tanner suddenly found himself staring at a photograph of Carly.

He frowned and shook his head. His brain must be befuddled, he thought. The child in the photograph couldn't be Carly. Flipping the picture over, he recognized and read his mother's precise handwriting. Tanner—five years old. Startled, he turned the picture over and studied it again.

The child in the photo definitely held a strong likeness to Carly; the smile was the same, the hair color matched, and the eyes... the eyes were the exact same shade of blue.

As he continued to stare at the face of the child, his brain suddenly supplied a logical and plausible reason for the resemblance.

Shock ricocheted through him at the simple explanation and for several minutes Tanner sat very still, his thoughts in a turmoil as he sorted through his memories in an attempt to dispute the reasoning.

But the more he thought about it, the more he began to believe the explanation had to be true. The twins were five years old and arithmetically the numbers were right. From the moment he'd seen the children he'd had the strong impression that Carly reminded him of someone. But he'd automatically assumed she seemed familiar because her father had been someone Tanner knew, a local resident.

Tanner's heart began to pound. If what he was thinking was true, then it explained Laura's reluctance to talk about their father. But if it was true, why hadn't she told him when she found out she was pregnant?

The answer came instantly. Because he'd called her Leanne that night, believing the woman he'd made love to was Leanne. Tanner rose from the chair and moved to stand at the small window with a partial view of the lake. He ran a hand through his hair and drew a steadying breath as he tried to control his galloping thoughts.

He had to think clearly, to cast his mind back to that unforgettable evening and try to recall exactly when and where he'd seen the girls that night.

Tanner slowly took himself back in time. He remembered the flight from Europe had been late, he'd missed one ferry and as a result he hadn't arrived at the lake until late afternoon. Billy had come running from the lodge to greet him but there had been no sign of Mac.

Tanner remembered walking through the dining room on his way upstairs and seeing Leanne—or had it been Laura?—setting the tables for the evening meal. He hadn't talked to her, he'd only smiled and waved in acknowledgement.

He'd assumed it was Leanne because of the way she was dressed. She'd been wearing a short summer dress, the kind that hugged every curve, the type Leanne generally wore. Laura, on the other hand, always wore shorts and T-shirts and was much more conservative, both in the way she dressed and behaved.

He'd sat up in Billy's room listening to his brother talk excitedly about his proposed trip to Europe, about the places he would visit. When he'd asked about Mac's reaction to his plans, Billy explained that he hadn't told his father about the trip, that he'd wanted to wait until Tanner arrived to give him moral support.

Mac had appeared in the doorway, greeting Tanner with a smile and handshake before informing them supper was ready. Billy had decided it was as good a time as any to tell Mac about his travel plans and so he'd blurted it out on the way downstairs.

Tanner couldn't recall seeing Laura or Leanne in the kitchen but then he'd been too preoccupied with the argument that had erupted between Billy and his father.

After a futile twenty minutes of arguing, Billy had stormed off leaving Tanner to try to calm his father down. But any attempt to placate him had failed. Mac hadn't listened, blaming Tanner for what he considered Billy's defection.

When the police arrived a short time later with the news of Billy's death, the hours that followed were a blur, and on their return from the hospital, Mac had launched another verbal attack.

Unable to take anymore, Tanner had walked out and he vaguely recalled passing a figure crouched on the stairs, a figure who had later followed him along the lakeshore.

He'd seen her approaching, at least he'd seen her silhouette in the moonlight, the feminine curves and tight-fitting outfit. He recalled shouting at Leanne to leave him alone, but she'd ignored him.

Could it have been Laura and not Leanne who'd followed him? At that point, he hadn't seen either of them for a year. Perhaps during that time Laura had started dressing more provocatively.

Tanner ran his hand over his face, trying to wipe away the feelings of fatigue and frustration descending on him. Was he simply jumping to wild conclusions? What proof did he have? Other than the fact that the children, especially Carly, held a strong resemblance to him, there was nothing concrete to go on.

Or was there? The question brought him up short. The woman he'd made love to that night had been a sensitive, caring and unselfish person, traits he'd seen demonstrated a number of times over the past week, traits he'd readily attributed to Laura.

The more Tanner thought about it, the more convinced he was that the suspicion taking root in his brain was indeed the truth. The twins were his own flesh and blood. *He was their father!*

With this thought came a cavalcade of emotions. Pride, joy, and an almost overwhelming feeling of love...but there was also anger, confusion and bitterness. Why hadn't she told him?

Should he confront her? Should he come out and ask her if the twins were his? If she denied it, what recourse did he have?

Tanner stood staring out across the lake watching the light of a new day slowly creep across the sky, and silently he made a vow that before this new day was over he would uncover the truth.

As Laura mixed the batter for the banana bran muffins, she stifled a yawn. She'd lain awake for most of the night thinking about Tanner. And during that long lonely night she'd decided that before Leanne made a slip and revealed something that would raise Tanner's suspicions, she would tell him the truth about the twins herself.

Perhaps in a secret corner of her heart she'd wanted the truth to come out—perhaps that had been the true reason she'd come to Moonbeam Lake.

There was no book or rule of etiquette that could help her deal with this situation, so throughout the night she'd played out numerous scenarios and countless conversations on exactly how she would tell Tanner he was the twins' father.

The first priority was to get Tanner alone with no chance of interruption. The kind of news she had to impart deserved a private setting.

But from the moment Laura had risen and dressed that morning, a swarm of butterflies had taken up residence in her stomach, and each time she heard footsteps or the sound of a voice the butterflies would begin to flutter madly inside her.

Getting Tanner alone wouldn't be easy and already Laura was wishing she'd taken the bull by the horns and told him last night, when he'd asked her whether the children saw their father.

As she scooped the batter into the muffin trays, she heard the door opening behind her, sending the butterflies into flight once more. She turned to see Tanner dressed in denim shorts and a white T-shirt and her awareness of him heightened.

"Morning," he said gruffly as he crossed to the counter and poured himself a cup of coffee.

"Morning," Laura responded, hearing the edge in his voice and wondering at the cause of it. Turning back to the task in hand, she willed her pulse to slow down, wishing she could control her reaction to this man. With great deliberation she finished filling the muffin trays and with one in each hand, carried them to the oven.

Tanner immediately appeared at her side and opened the oven door.

"Thanks," Laura said as she set the trays on the shelves.

"How long do they take?" Tanner asked.

"Twenty-five minutes," Laura picked up a dish towel from a nearby chair, sure that he must hear the frantic pounding of her heart.

"I doubt I'll be back by then," Tanner said in a tone that sent a shiver down her spine.

But before she could ask where he was going, the kitchen door swung open and the twins, Craig in the lead, came running in at full speed. Tanner immediately bent down and scooped Craig up in his arms lifting him high over his head.

"Whoa there, son! Where's the fire?" Tanner asked, as he smiled up at the child.

Laura felt her heart skid to a halt at his words. Was she imagining it or had there been a different ring to the way he'd said "son." Laura darted a guilty glance at Tanner but although she saw nothing untoward in his expression, somehow she couldn't dispel the feeling that something was wrong.

"Me too! Me too!" Carly declared in a loud voice.

"Okay, squirt," Tanner said, laughter and affection in his tone as he set Craig on the floor. He lifted Carly high above his head and she squealed with delight.

"What's going on in here?" The question came from Mac who joined them in the kitchen.

"We're playing," Craig announced.

"And I'm flying. See?" said Carly, and Tanner obligingly swooped her around once more before setting her down on the floor.

"Breakfast's on the table, you two," said Laura, aware that her chances of getting an opportunity to talk to Tanner any time soon were slim.

She'd just have to try later. Perhaps if she suggested to Mac that he take the children fishing, she would have an opportunity to talk to Tanner alone.

"I'll eat when I get back," Tanner said, effectively breaking into her thoughts. "I'm going to pop over and see Leanne."

"Can we come with you?" the children asked in unison.

"No," Tanner quickly replied. "I won't be long." He set his empty cup in the sink and headed toward the door.

Laura felt her heart go out to the children as their smiles quickly faded in response to Tanner's rebuff. And suddenly the question that had kept her awake most of the night popped into her head. Would telling Tanner he was the twins' father really be in their best interests?

The twins had become very fond of him, yes, but Tanner's career would undoubtedly take him away for long periods of time, not an ideal situation—especially where children were concerned.

And the fact that he was going to see Leanne cut her to the quick, leaving her wondering if he'd made an arrangement with Leanne the previous night when he'd walked her back to the cabin. Perhaps Tanner *was* interested in pursuing a relationship with Leanne, Laura thought, remembering with a pang his reaction when her cousin had arrived yesterday.

Though Irene had indicated Leanne was interested in someone in Hawaii, that didn't mean a great deal. Besides, Leanne had always had a thing for Tanner. That's why Laura hadn't told her cousin all that happened the night Billy died.

Suddenly Laura's resolve to tell Tanner the truth began to weaken, undermined, she knew, by the questions and speculations she'd been indulging in. Perhaps coming back to Moonbeam Lake and stirring up the past had been a mistake after all.

The oven timer began to buzz noisily, effectively breaking into Laura's depressing thoughts. Putting on the oven gloves, she removed the muffins and set them on a cooling tray.

"Good morning, everyone," Irene said as she appeared in the kitchen doorway. "Am I too late for breakfast?"

"Hi, Grandma!" Carly said.

"Hi, Grandma!" Craig echoed.

"Of course you're not too late." Laura reached into the cupboard for a coffee cup.

"Good morning, Irene," Mac said, as he rose to pull out a chair for her.

"Thank you." Irene kissed each child before sitting down.

"I just took these out of the oven," Laura said as she set a cup of coffee and a plate of muffins in front of her mother.

"They smell wonderful." Irene smiled at Laura. "I just passed Tanner a few minutes ago. Where's he going in such a hurry?" she asked.

"He's gone to see Leanne," Mac said, and at his words Irene threw a questioning glance at Laura.

"Who wants to go fishing after breakfast?" Mac asked, but his question was met with silence.

"Carly, Craig. Mac's talking to you," Laura prompted them.

"If you don't feel like going fishing today, that's okay," Mac said kindly. "I should really drive into town and see Doc Morro. Want to come for the ride?"

The twins' expression changed to smiles once more. A trip into town was a treat indeed. They glanced at

Laura who smiled and nodded her assent. "I need a few things from the store. I'll make Mac a list and give you each a dollar to spend," she told them.

"All right!" Craig said, grinning at his sister now.

"Would you mind if I tag along?" Irene asked as she buttered a muffin.

"We'd be delighted to have you. Right, kids?"

"Right!" they chorused.

Laura made up her list and after Mac, Craig, Carly and her mother departed, she busied herself clearing away the dishes in the dining room.

The lodge seemed unusually quiet and Laura turned the radio on to fill the void as she washed the breakfast dishes. After restoring the kitchen to order, she made her way upstairs to the bedrooms to make beds and tidy the children's room.

As she gathered the books up off the floor and rescued Carly's stuffed bear from behind her bed, Laura found her thoughts switching to Tanner and Leanne. Would they return together all smiles and announce that she wasn't going to Toronto after all?

Pain, sharp and intense, caught her unawares and Laura sat down on the bed hugging Carly's bear in a vain attempt to alleviate the ache in her chest.

She should never have come back. The foolish dream she'd harboured for so long—that for her and the children there would be a happy-ever-after—was just that, a foolish dream.

"I've been looking for you."

Laura gasped in surprise and glanced up to see Tanner standing in the doorway, staring down at her with eyes almost black with anger and something more. Was it pain?

"Just when were you planning on telling me the twins were mine? Or were you going to sneak back to Vancouver without saying a word?"

Laura gasped in shock at his words and recoiled as if she had been struck.

"How..." she began, then broke off realizing that what she had hoped to avoid had in fact happened. Bravely she met his penetrating gaze as the shock of learning he'd uncovered the truth quickly wore off, leaving in its wake a feeling of relief, relief that she no longer had to live in the shadow of her deception.

Tanner was surprised at the depth of his anger. When he'd gone to talk to Leanne, he'd acknowledged that there was still a small part of him ready and willing to believe he was mistaken.

Though the twins resembled him and there was a possibility they were his, he'd found himself wondering if he was simply indulging in wishful thinking, that his dream to one day have a family of his own had influenced and distorted his thinking.

When he'd arrived at the cabin and Leanne answered his knock, he hadn't really been sure just what he should say, or how he would ask the question burning a hole in his brain.

After exchanging a few polite remarks, he'd opted for a straightforward approach.

"Leanne, this might seem like a dumb question," he'd begun, "but where were you the night Billy died?"

She'd looked at him as if he were out of his mind and for a fleeting second he'd thought she was going to give him the answer he suddenly realized he didn't want—that she'd been with him.

"I went to the movies. Why?" she asked in a puzzled tone.

"And after the movies?" He ignored her question.

"I got a ride back with a couple of the kids staying at the lake. We noticed a police car at the railway abutment. We didn't know what had happened. Anyway, I got dropped off at the end of the driveway and walked home from there. That's when my mother told me about Billy—" She stopped. "I don't understand. What's this all about, Tanner?"

"Nothing, nothing that concerns you," he'd told her and without another word he'd taken his leave.

Throughout the walk back to the lodge, his emotions had gone from one extreme to the other, from feeling absolutely ecstatic to quiet, blind fury.

It was true! Leanne had confirmed that Laura had been the one he'd made love to that night and in the midst of death and emotional turmoil she had conceived a life... two lives.

"Just how long were you planning on keeping it a secret?" He bit out the question. "If I hadn't been looking through old photographs last night, you would probably have left here at the end of the summer without saying a word, wouldn't you?" he asked, his voice thick with anger.

Laura opened her mouth to answer but Tanner wasn't finished.

"I'm not sure I shouldn't hate you for what you've done," he hurried on. "You deliberately deceived me that night, Laura. Why? Were you getting some kind of kick out of pretending to be Leanne? Was that it?"

Again he didn't wait for a reply. "And if that wasn't bad enough, you continued the deceit, not only depriving me of the knowledge that I had fathered twins, but depriving my father of his grandchildren."

Laura fought back the tears suddenly threatening to fall. She knew she deserved his anger, but that didn't make it any easier to deal with.

"You said something about photographs," said Laura at a loss to understand their significance. "What photographs are you talking about?" she asked.

"I went up to the attic last night," he told her, his tone even, his anger obviously spent. "I was looking through old photos Mac had hidden away when I came across one of Carly, or at least I thought it was Carly, until I read my mother's handwriting on the back. It was a picture of me . . . but the likeness to Carly was striking and that's when I put two and two together."

"I see," Laura said softly.

"But I wanted to be absolutely sure. That's why I went to see Leanne this morning. When I asked her where she was the night Billy died, she told me she'd gone to the movies."

Laura took a steadying breath. "What do you intend to do?" she asked, lifting her eyes to meet his.

"There's only one solution that I can see," Tanner said, his eyes boring into hers in unmistakable challenge. "We should get married."

Chapter Ten

Laura felt her mouth drop open in astonishment at Tanner's announcement. She was glad she was already sitting down for she knew without a shadow of a doubt that had she been standing she would surely have fainted.

She swallowed convulsively. "Married?" she said, her voice little more than a squeak.

"Yes," came the prompt reply. "I *am* the twins' father, and marriage would be the least traumatic way for the children to begin accepting me as their father. I don't think they'll object to the new arrangement, and later when they're old enough to understand, we can tell them the truth."

"I . . . well, I mean . . ." She stumbled over the words still trying to recover from the shock of his proposal. No, she amended silently—it wasn't a proposal—more like an ultimatum.

"Anybody home?" a voice called out from downstairs, effectively cutting through the tension shimmering in the air between them.

"It's Leanne." Laura rose to her feet, welcoming the intrusion. She was at a loss to know how to answer Tanner and she needed time to think, time to sort out her feelings, time to decide what was right for the children.

Laura crossed to the doorway, but Tanner stood his ground, deliberately blocking her way. She lifted her gaze to meet his and as their glances collided, her muscles tensed at the indefinable look she saw in the depths of his eyes.

For a fleeting moment she thought he was going to kiss her and she was overwhelmed with anticipation.

"Hello! Laura! Is anyone there?" Leanne's voice, louder this time, echoed up the stairwell, breaking the spell.

Laura squeezed past Tanner but his hand came out to capture her. A shiver of sensation shot along her arm and it was all she could do to meet his penetrating gaze, afraid he would see the awareness in her eyes.

"I have some business to take care of in town today. I'll expect your answer tonight," he said softly, almost threateningly, before he released her.

"Coming!" Laura called as she hurried along the landing and down the stairs, relieved to make her escape.

"There you are," Leanne said, a hint of exasperation in her tone. "Where is everybody this morning?"

"Mom and the twins went with Mac into town to run a few errands," Laura said. "Come into the kitchen and I'll make a fresh pot of coffee."

"I'd forgotten how dead this place is." Leanne looked gorgeous in a cotton sundress made from a colorful Hawaiian print.

"It's peaceful and relaxing," Laura countered, though the past week had been anything but, she thought, as she filled the carafe with water and proceeded to make coffee.

"I don't know how you can stand it," Leanne continued as she paced the kitchen. "Give me a mall with lots of interesting shops and I'm in heaven."

Laura laughed. "Mother tells me there's a new man in your life."

Leanne smiled. "Carl is such a sweetheart," she said, affection in her tone. "He owns a chain of jewelry stores. Look what he gave me for my birthday." She thrust her right hand toward Laura to show off a ring of emeralds and diamonds.

"It's beautiful," Laura said, thinking fleetingly that she'd never in her life received a gift of any kind from a man.

"He's in Toronto right now," Leanne explained.

"So that's the reason you're headed there," Laura said teasingly and at her words a blush crept across Leanne's cheeks.

"Actually he did ask me to marry him when he gave me the ring," her cousin said somewhat boastfully.

"And you refused?" Laura said.

"I told him it was much too soon," Leanne replied. "I mean, my divorce only came through a month ago."

"When did he propose to you?" Laura asked.

"A week ago," said Leanne. "It was so romantic." She sighed. "He took me out in his yacht and we were having dinner by candlelight when suddenly he told me he loved me and wanted to marry me."

Laura glanced at her cousin who appeared to be staring into space, her eyes glowing. "Do you love him?" Laura asked.

Leanne blinked several times before turning to Laura. "Yes . . . yes, I do," she said, almost as if she'd just realized it herself.

"Then why are you stalling?" Laura said, trying not to think about her own situation. Tanner had suggested marriage, but his proposal had been far from romantic, and there had been no ring, no declaration of love.

"You're absolutely right. I am stalling," said Leanne as she turned to Laura. "Do you know, I was actually flying to Toronto to tell Carl I'd changed my mind, that I wanted to accept his proposal, when suddenly I got scared. The only reason I came here was because it gave me an excuse to avoid Carl for a few more days." She pulled Laura into her arms and hugged her. "Thanks, Laura, you helped me see that I truly love Carl and I really do want to marry him." She spun away and headed for the door, then stopped. "Which ferry is your mother planning to take back to the mainland?"

"The two o'clock," Laura said a little dazedly. "She should be back from the store any time now." Her words were followed by the sound of a car pulling up to the lodge. "That might even be them now."

"Good, because I'm going with her," Leanne said resolutely and Laura felt a little stab of envy at Leanne's obvious happiness at the decision she'd made.

The car was indeed Mac's, and minutes later the twins appeared, each carrying a bag of goodies and chattering nineteen to the dozen about their trip into town.

Laura barely had an opportunity to talk to her mother. Now that she had made up her mind about

Carl, Leanne was like a bulldozer with a cause and Irene was quickly hustled off to prepare for their departure.

Half an hour later Irene and Leanne, packed and ready to leave, dropped by to say their farewells. The twins kissed and hugged their grandmother and aunt, and Laura bid her mother and Leanne goodbye, frustrated by the fact that she hadn't had a chance to tell her mother that Tanner had uncovered the truth about the twins or that he'd suggested they get married.

"Where's Tanner?" Carly asked after Irene had driven away.

"He said he had some business to take care of in town," Laura said, pleased that her voice betrayed none of the inner turmoil she experienced at the mention of his name.

"I wonder why he didn't come with us?" Mac said with a frown.

After lunch Mac and the twins went fishing while Laura put several loads of laundry through the washer and dryer and finished the job of peeling and cutting the potatoes for french fries. Hamburger patties were already made and in the fridge in readiness for the evening meal.

Lack of sleep and the strain of trying not to think about Tanner and the decision he was forcing her to make had brought on a thundering headache. What answer would she give him when he returned?

As she mixed up a batch of iced tea, she found herself wondering if her decision would have been any easier had he spoken of loving her and wanting her to be his wife.

Laura shook her head and sighed. She'd always longed to be loved, to be wanted and needed, pampered and cared for... romanced by the man of her dreams.

No man had ever sent her flowers—not even a single long-stemmed rose. No man had ever given her a piece of jewelry—not even the smallest of trinkets. No man had ever offered to share anything with her—not even a bowl of fresh strawberries and whipped cream.

While those were the kinds of romantic things a man might do for the woman he loved, they only ever happened on television shows or movies or books.

Laura was suddenly jolted out of her daydream when the children and Mac returned from their fishing expedition.

"Look what we caught." Craig held up a good-sized fish.

"Is Tanner back yet?" Carly asked as she stood next to her brother, fish in hand.

"No, Tanner isn't back," Laura said, unable to keep the annoyance from her voice.

Mac threw her a puzzled glance and then ushered the twins off to clean their fish.

Laura silently scolded herself for taking her frustrations out on the children. But she was no nearer to making a decision about whether or not to marry Tanner than she had been that morning.

She knew that if the decision was up to the twins, their answer would be an immediate and unqualified yes. But she also knew that their decision would be strongly influenced by the fact that during the past week, Carly and Craig had grown to love the man who was their father.

And Laura knew all too well how easy it was to love Tanner. Hadn't she been in love with him from the moment she'd laid eyes on him the first summer she'd spent at Moonbeam Lake when she was only thirteen?

Laura drew a startled breath. Could it be true? Was she still in love with Tanner?

She closed her eyes and blinked away the tears suddenly welling up in her eyes. Biting down on the softness of her lower lip, she silently acknowledged what she'd been trying so desperately to deny since the moment Tanner had walked back into her life.

She loved him, had never stopped loving him. Her love for him had simply lain dormant over the years waiting for his return, kept alive by the presence of his children.

"Tanner's back! Tanner's back!"

Laura heard the chant and glanced outside to see Tanner sitting in the passenger seat of a pickup truck. Her breath caught in her throat as she watched his long lean body emerge from the cab. Her reaction to him was easily explained now; it was simply the reaction of a woman in love when she sees the man who is the keeper of her heart.

Tears blurred her vision once more as Tanner bent to scoop Carly and Craig into his arms. Their smiles matched his as they clung to him and in that moment Laura knew that she could no more deprive the children of the love of their father, or their father the love of his children, than she could fly to the moon.

Tanner felt his heart swell with joy and love as he carried the twins inside. He'd spent the day in town dealing with a number of things, which included returning the car he'd rented at the airport when he'd arrived over a week ago.

He'd spent most of the day thinking and planning, all on the assumption, of course, that Laura would accept his suggestion that they get married. He wanted to become a big part of their lives, to spend as much time with the twins as possible, and he'd convinced himself marriage was the only way he could accomplish that goal.

While he was in town, he'd contacted a real estate agent in Vancouver and had given him a description of the size and style of house he was in the market for. And he'd also asked the agent to locate a property in the downtown area that could be set up as a gallery and photography studio combined.

But finding a house in Vancouver or one of the outlying areas, was the first priority. He felt sure that moving into a home of their own would be far less disruptive for the twins, especially if it could be done before the start of the school year.

As the day progressed, the anger he'd felt at Laura's deception vanished and instead of thinking about the past and what he'd missed, he'd turned his attention to the future. Ideas and plans began to bubble to the surface, but as each new idea emerged, Tanner found his thoughts continually returning to Laura. What would her answer be?

After snagging a ride back to the lake from an old friend in town, Tanner was surprised to discover that the emotion taking precedence over all the others was fear. Fear that Laura would turn him down.

When the twins greeted him with such warmth and enthusiasm, he felt somewhat encouraged, for a while at least, but as the evening wore on, his anxiety steadily grew.

Tanner couldn't seem to shake the feeling that there was a great deal more at stake here than he was ready to admit, but it wasn't until the children were in bed that he had the chance to confront Laura.

Mac was sitting in his favorite chair in the living room, watching a program on television and Laura was alone in the kitchen when Tanner came downstairs after putting the twins to bed.

"We have to talk." At his words, a shiver of apprehension and something more danced across Laura's nerve endings.

Slowly, deliberately, she dried her hands and turned to face him, acknowledging his words with a nod. From the moment he'd returned from town, she'd sensed his impatience but there had been no opportunity to talk to him until now.

"I'll tell Mac we're going for a walk," Tanner said. "That way we won't be disturbed."

Again Laura nodded and Tanner turned and headed to the living room. Catching a glimpse of her reflection in the window, she suddenly wished she'd thought to pay a visit to her bedroom to brush her hair and perhaps add a touch of lipstick to her mouth.

Reaching up, she pulled the combs from her hair and tucked them into the pocket of her shorts. She shook her hair loose and silently chastised herself for thinking Tanner would even notice.

"All set?" Tanner asked as he poked his head into the kitchen.

Tanner held the door for her and as Laura slid past him, her body brushed briefly against his, sending her pulse skyrocketing.

Laura picked up her pace and hurried outside, wishing she could control her body's reaction to him, yet knowing it was as impossible as walking on water.

The evening air blowing gently off the lake was cool and refreshing. Avoiding the path to the jetty where several teenagers had congregated, Tanner directed her instead to the path that led to the sandy lakeshore.

The sound of laughter drifted toward them on the breeze and mingled with the softer sound of waves lapping on the shore. Laura came to a halt at the water's edge and as Tanner drew up beside her she felt her heartbeat accelerate and her skin tingle in anticipation.

They stood for a long moment staring out across the water, which was shimmering like a blanket of silver in the glow of twilight. It was Tanner who broke the silence.

"What's your answer, Laura?" he asked and there was no mistaking the tension in his voice.

Laura swallowed the lump in her throat. "Are you sure marriage is what you want, Tanner?" she managed to ask. "You could come and see the children as often as you wanted. I wouldn't deny you that right," she went on, all the while wishing he would take her in his arms and tell her that the reason he wanted to marry her was because he loved her and not just because he wanted to be with the children.

"They're my children, Laura. I don't just want visiting rights," he said in an icy tone. "I want to spend time with them every day. To be there when they need me, to make them laugh and to comfort them when they cry—to tuck them in bed and kiss them good-night, every night. I want to be a full-time father."

Any hope that he might have feelings for her vanished with every word he spoke. The twins were obviously all that was important to Tanner, and with this realization came a pain so intense Laura thought someone had taken a dagger and thrust it through her heart.

But to say *no* would be to deny the twins the father they already adored and that was something she couldn't bring herself to do. Tanner would be a wonderful father, of that she had no doubt, and what could possible be wrong with marrying the only man she'd ever loved?

"If you're sure that's what you want," Laura said hesitantly, ignoring the ache in her chest and trying with difficulty to keep her voice from trembling.

"Is that a yes?" Tanner demanded, an edge of anxiety in his tone as his hand came out to turn her to face him.

"Yes," Laura said softly, lifting her gaze to meet his, and for a fleeting moment she saw an emotion flicker in the depth of his eyes that she couldn't quite define.

"Thank you," she heard him say, and there was no mistaking the relief in his voice. Suddenly she found herself pulled into his arms, her face nestled in the curve of his neck. "You won't regret it," he said softly into her hair, but Laura was lost in a sea of sensation as the rich male scent of him assaulted her senses, sending the delicious thrill of desire racing through her.

Laura's hair felt like silk against his cheek and her perfume reminded him of lilacs in spring. His relief that she'd said yes was overwhelming, but as he held her to him, he was astonished to discover that he was reluctant to let her go.

Desire, sharp and unexpected, splintered through him and he found himself tossed back in time to the night so long ago when he'd made love to Laura.

He hadn't planned to kiss her. Kissing her had been the furthest thing from his mind that night. But fate had had other plans, and the moment his mouth had touched hers, he remembered feeling as if he'd suddenly been blasted into orbit.

She'd been like fire and ice—one minute burning with unbridled passion and the next melting beneath him like an ice sculpture. No woman had ever driven him to such heights of passion—and no woman had given of herself with such generosity and total abandonment.

And in those earth-shattering moments when he'd wished he had died instead of Billy, she had given him a precious gift, and restored his will to carry on.

Laura pulled free of Tanner's embrace, unable to bear the pain any longer. He was merely acting out of gratitude, nothing more, and suddenly she wondered if she wasn't making the biggest mistake of her life.

"I'm tired, I think I'll go in now." Laura kept her gaze averted, all the while wishing Tanner would take her back into the warm haven of his arms.

"I'd like to tell the twins as soon as possible," Tanner said.

"Whatever you decide is fine with me." Laura was already backing away.

"How about tomorrow at breakfast?" he went on.

"Fine." Laura made her escape.

Back at the lodge she was relieved to hear voices coming from the living room. Mac was either still watching television or asleep in front of the set.

Grabbing a towel from the linen closet, she filled the bathtub and, locking the bathroom door this time, she lowered herself into the soothing water, trying not to think about what lay ahead. She'd given Tanner her decision and she'd abide by it, but that didn't stop her from wishing and hoping and dreaming.

How different everything would have been had Tanner wanted to marry her because he loved her. How wonderful everything would have been had he asked her for a date, taken her out to dinner, danced with her until midnight, then kissed her deeply and passionately on the doorstep and asked her to marry him.

But it was not to be and so she pushed aside her romantic notions and hung on to the simple but telling truth that after all was said and done, she was marrying the man she loved almost more than life itself.

Chapter Eleven

Laura was tense and more than a little nervous the next morning as she waited for everyone to come down for breakfast. Mac was the first to appear, and after a friendly greeting he poured himself a cup of coffee and sat down at the table. Minutes later the twins and Tanner arrived and Laura flipped the last of the pancakes she'd been making onto a plate, setting it on the table.

Glancing up, she met Tanner's gaze and her breath caught in her throat at the strange look that flickered briefly in the depths of his blue eyes.

She gathered up all her courage and strength as he came around the table to stand beside her.

"Okay kids, Dad. Listen up. We have something important to tell you," Tanner began.

Mac threw a startled glance at his son, and the twins, their breakfasts momentarily forgotten, looked up at Laura, their eyes wide with interest.

"Laura and I are going to be married," Tanner announced and as he spoke he put his arm around Laura's waist and flashed a smile at her.

Laura felt her face grow warm under his gaze and she quickly darted a look at the twins, wondering what their reaction to the news would be.

"Well, I'll be!" Mac said as he pushed his chair back and stood up, grinning in obvious delight at Laura and Tanner. "That's wonderful . . . just wonderful," he exclaimed. "What do you say, kids?" He turned to Carly and Craig, who were exchanging questioning glances.

Craig turned to Tanner. "Does that mean you'll be our daddy?" he asked, his tone serious.

"Yes . . . I'll be your daddy." Tanner confirmed and Laura held her breath for a moment in anticipation of their response.

The twins' faces instantly lit up.

"You'll really be our very own daddy?" This time it was Carly who asked the question. Her eyes, so like Tanner's and as big as the pancake on her plate, regarded him intently.

"If you'll have me. I'd be very proud to be your daddy,"

Laura heard the catch in Tanner's voice as he responded.

Carly quickly glanced at her brother and together they let out a whoop of joy. Breakfast was forgotten as they scrambled down from their chairs and raced toward Tanner.

Laura didn't know whether to laugh or cry as the children danced at their feet in a frenzy of excitement. Tanner lifted Carly into his arms, accepting her exuberant hug and congratulatory kiss with a tenderness that brought tears to Laura's eyes.

Taking Carly from him, Laura hugged her smiling daughter and watched as Tanner lifted his son into his arms and accepted the boy's fierce embrace.

Mac, too, joined in the celebration, extending his hand and offering Laura and Tanner his congratulations. After the initial excitement was over, the children returned to their seats and between mouthfuls began asking questions.

"When are you going to get married?" Craig asked.

Laura opened her mouth to answer, but Tanner did the honors. "As soon as possible," he said and at his words Laura felt her pulse pick up speed.

"When's that?" Carly asked, seconds before she stuffed a wedge of pancake into her mouth.

"How about the first of September? That sounds like a good day to me," Tanner said, obviously enjoying himself. "What do you think, Laura?"

Laura blinked and tried with difficulty to find her voice. "Ah...well...yes, that's fine," she mumbled, realizing with a sudden sense of panic that the date Tanner mentioned was only a few weeks away.

"Where will we live? Here or at Grandma Irene's?" Craig asked.

"Well," Tanner began. "I don't know if there'll be enough room at your grandmother's. What do you think?"

"It's not very big," Carly said. "You'd have to sleep with Mom, unless you want to share with Craig and me."

At Carly's words Laura almost choked. Across the table Mac began to chuckle and Tanner appeared to be trying his darnedest not to laugh.

"I'll have to think about that," Tanner said, amusement evident in his voice. Laura saw the glimmer of laughter in his eyes and had to fight the urge to throw something at him.

"This is a red-letter day indeed," Mac said a little while later when the twins had gone upstairs to brush their teeth. "Laura, I can't tell you how much it means to me to know that I'll be able to look on those two rascals of yours as my grandchildren. And who knows, one day you may decide to have another." He shot her a teasing grin.

"Hey, let's take this one step at a time, Dad," Tanner said evenly.

"It's a day of new beginnings," Mac continued, emotion clouding his voice now. "And Son, I think it's time you and I put the past behind us. I hope you can forgive a stubborn and foolish old man."

Laura felt her throat clog with emotion as she glimpsed Tanner's incredulous reaction to his father's words. He seemed at a loss for words and for a moment Laura saw a glimmer of tears in his eyes.

"There's nothing to forgive. I love you, Dad," Tanner said.

"I love you, too, Son," Mac replied, and as Laura watched the two men embrace, a tear spilled over to trace a path down her cheek.

She turned to the sink, quickly wiping the moisture from her face with the back of her hand, trying not to think how perfect everything would be if only Tanner loved her.

Once they were married they would be a family, but while that thought brought a warm glow to her heart, Laura couldn't help wishing Tanner had said those three little words to her. But she knew she was wishing for the moon.

From the day the twins learned that Tanner was to become their father, the children seemed to undergo a change. Every spare moment they had they spent with Tanner, and if they weren't with Tanner, they were with Tanner and Mac.

They continued to help Laura set the tables in the dining room and managed to carry out the chores she assigned them, but Laura began to feel as though she was somehow competing with Tanner for their love and attention.

The week proved to be one of the busiest of the season and Laura hardly had a minute to herself. Temperatures soared, bringing hot sunny days and sticky sleepless nights.

Tanner was teaching the twins to swim and each day Laura watched as they grew more confident in the water. Somehow she couldn't help feeling a little resentful at how quickly the children learned to float under his tuition, especially when they'd balked at her efforts to teach them shortly after their arrival at the lake.

Tanner appeared to have endless patience and Laura couldn't help but admire the loving, understanding way he handled them. Whenever he had to discipline them, he rarely had to raise his voice.

It was late Friday afternoon and Laura was in the kitchen putting the finishing touches to the evening meal when Tanner joined her.

"Got a minute?" he asked.

"Sure," Laura answered, ignoring the way her pulse had jumped at the sight of him.

"Ah... I was wondering if you'd like to go out for dinner tonight?"

Startled, Laura brought her eyes to meet his, but his expression was unreadable. "I'm sure the children would love to," she said politely.

"I'm not asking the twins. I'm asking you," he told her, a hint of annoyance in his tone.

"Oh... well." Laura felt her face grow hot with embarrassment.

"You've been working like a Trojan all week. You deserve a break. I thought you might enjoy a night out," Tanner went on. "The twins and Mac agreed."

"Oh... I see," Laura said, trying with difficulty to hide the pleasure she felt at his thoughtfulness.

"Say yes," he instructed her. "If you don't, not only will you disappoint me, but you'll also disappoint three other people who shall remain nameless." He nodded his head toward the window.

Laura frowned, then followed Tanner's gaze to where Mac and the twins stood watching them from the porch.

"Well, I certainly wouldn't want to disappoint anyone," Laura said, keeping her tone light, all the while feeling as giddy as a schoolgirl who'd been asked on her very first date.

"Good," Tanner replied. "I made a reservation at The Hollow for seven o'clock." He glanced at his watch. "I'll meet you on the porch in an hour."

At six-thirty on the dot, Tanner, wearing gray cotton slacks and a sky-blue, short-sleeved chambray shirt, stood on the porch waiting for Laura. He was surprised to discover that he felt nervous about the evening ahead.

Since the night she'd given him her answer to his proposal, he hadn't been able to forget the way she'd felt in his arms. When she'd pulled free of the embrace, he'd been unprepared for the feeling of emptiness that enveloped him. He'd watched her walk away, and wondered why the joy he'd experienced just moments before had suddenly deserted him.

The past week had been hectic for everyone and, other than at mealtimes, he hadn't even had an opportunity to talk to Laura alone, a circumstance he'd found infinitely frustrating.

The idea of a date...spending an evening with her away from the lodge had come to him out of the blue. But he rationalized that they had the wedding arrangements to discuss and the date they'd agreed on was only weeks away.

Suddenly his musings were brought to a halt when the screen door opened and Laura appeared. Beautiful, absolutely beautiful, Tanner thought as she joined him on the porch.

Her hair fell softly around her face to frame her delicate features. She wore a minimum of makeup, only a touch of blusher to accentuate her high cheekbones, a dab of eye shadow that brought out the green in her eyes and a trace of lipstick in a shade that made her lips look full and sensual and decidedly kissable.

A pink V-necked sweater gently hugged her breasts and showed off her lightly tanned skin to perfection. And defining the swell of her hips, a straight navy skirt, stopping just above her knees, revealed legs that were long and shapely.

Tanner felt as if he'd been hit by a speeding train and it took every ounce of self-control not to haul her into his arms and taste the promise of sweetness he could see on her lips.

"You look pretty, Mommy," Carly said as she played with Craig on the swings.

"Doesn't she look pretty, Tanner?" Craig asked.

"She does indeed," Tanner said with a sigh.

"Thank you," Laura said, smiling at the twins and trying to ignore the warmth spreading through her at Tanner's words as well as trying to quell the butterflies fluttering in her stomach. For a moment she'd thought she saw a look of desire flash in the depths of Tanner's eyes, but it was gone before she could be sure.

For the past hour she'd been fussing and fretting about what she should wear. She kept telling herself it wasn't really a date she was going on, but the tension throbbing at her temples and the queasy feeling in her stomach refused to go away.

"Let's get this show on the road," Tanner said as he escorted her down the steps to his father's car.

"Have a good time," Mac called after them.

Laura sat in silence for several minutes, trying to think of a safe topic of conversation. She glanced at Tanner through lowered lashes and her heart tightened inside her breast as she feasted her eyes on his handsome profile.

His black hair glistened like polished ebony and the breeze flowing through the open windows caused several strands to fall across his forehead, giving him a raw sexuality that tugged sharply at her insides. The earthy scent of leather and spice teased her nostrils, stirring her senses and making it almost impossible to think or breathe.

"It's been a hectic week," Tanner said, breaking the silence.

"Yes, it has."

"I hope this hot spell is over soon," Tanner commented.

"I heard on the radio that it's supposed to last another week."

"Really."

Laura curled her fingers around her purse and gazed outside at the passing scene, wishing now she'd never agreed to come. She felt awkward and unsure of herself, convinced that she was no match for the women Tanner usually went out with.

Undoubtedly they were incredibly beautiful and highly intelligent career women who could talk about anything and everything. Laura felt like a timid country mouse, totally lacking in sophistication and as boring as a stalk of celery.

Fifteen minutes later when Tanner drove the car into an empty space in the restaurant's parking lot, Laura was as tightly strung as the strings of a violin.

"Are you as nervous as I am?" Tanner asked when he turned off the engine.

Laura threw a startled glance at him, thinking that he might be making fun of her, but his expression was serious. She licked lips that were dry. "I am a little nervous, yes," she admitted shyly.

"I have an idea," he went on. "Why don't we pretend that we've only just met and I've invited you to join me for dinner so that we can get to know each other better."

At this words Laura felt her anxiety slip away. His confession that he, too, was nervous had surprised her. She'd been worried that Tanner would spend the evening asking her questions about the past, wanting to know her reasons for not telling him about the twins. But it was obvious that she was mistaken, that he didn't have that in mind at all, and Laura quickly made the decision to meet him halfway.

"All right," she said softly and felt a rush of pleasure when Tanner smiled.

The tone of the evening was set as the maitre d' showed them to their table outside on the tiled courtyard. Laura felt a giddy sense of happiness sweep over her as she took her seat opposite Tanner.

A bud vase with a single yellow rose was the table's decoration and as she glanced out across the meadow beyond the patio, Laura knew she would never forget this night.

The salmon entrées they ordered were delicately flavored with herbs and spices and quite simply delicious. And the white wine Tanner chose as an accompaniment to their meal was cool and crisp on her tongue.

Tanner was charming and attentive, making her laugh by telling her stories about some of the people he'd met and places he'd visited.

She in turn made him laugh with stories about the restaurant and some of the problems she'd encountered. They discussed a wide range of topics, discovering they had similar tastes in music and books. They argued companionably about what they considered the best movie they'd seen and by the time coffee was served, Laura found herself wishing the evening would last forever.

As the sun slowly set and the air cooled, Laura wonder if Tanner was as reluctant as she to leave.

When the waiter brought the check, Laura rose. "Excuse me. I think I'll powder my nose before we head back."

As Tanner stood, he watched Laura make her way through the glass doors and across the restaurant's main dining room, and silently acknowledged that he was sorry the evening was drawing to a close.

All through the meal he'd found himself constantly captivated by Laura's smile and the sound of her laughter. He began to wish the restaurant had a dance floor, as the urge to touch her and hold her in his arms slowly became a torment.

He found it difficult to believe that in only a few short weeks his whole life had been turned upside down. When he'd come home to Moonbeam Lake to make peace with his father, he hadn't expected to achieve that goal quite so quickly. He had Laura and the children to thank for that.

Nor had he expected to discover that he had a family of his own. A feeling of love and pride washed over him as he thought of the twins. How quickly he had grown to love them, and how empty his life would be without them . . . and without Laura. The thought brought him up short.

He'd been haunted by the memory of the warm, generous, incredibly sensual woman he'd made love to that night six years ago. There had been something about her, some indefinable quality that had reached out to him, leaving an indelible mark on his soul.

And the moment he'd realized Laura was the woman responsible for bringing him back from the edge of despair, everything that had puzzled him about the encounter suddenly started to make sense.

The more he thought about it, the more he was convinced that had he not been going through an emotional wringer, he never would have mistaken Laura for Leanne. But the fact that he had made the error, an error Laura had been aware of, had undoubtedly affected the decisions she'd been forced to make.

The anger he'd felt when he'd learned he was the twins' father had been sharp and very real. The fact that he'd missed some of the most important years of their lives had cut him to the quick, and selfishly he'd wanted to claim his rightful place as their father.

Not for a moment had he stopped to think about what Laura might want, or need. He'd simply seen marriage as a means to an end, but suddenly with startling clarity he realized that not only did he want to lay claim to the children, he wanted to lay claim to Laura, too.

Why? Because he was in love with her! Totally, irrevocably in love with her—and had been since that unforgettable night six years ago.

Tanner closed his eyes for a moment, rejoicing in the knowledge, and wondering why he had taken so long to recognize it.

The tragedy of losing his brother, the accompanying grief and emotional turmoil generated by his father's reaction to Billy's death had created an intensely stressful situation.

As a result, the feelings Laura had aroused in him that fateful night had been swept aside and ultimately buried in the confusion and chaos that ensued.

And all this time Laura had faced and dealt admirably with a situation any woman would have found challenging. She'd proven without a doubt that she was resourceful and strong, and more than capable of looking after herself and the twins.

Why then had she agreed to marry him? It was a question that was suddenly of vital importance—a question he desperately needed to know the answer to.

"I'm sorry if I've kept you waiting, Tanner, but I had to pop into the kitchen and offer my compliments to the chef," Laura said when she returned.

"What? Oh...sorry. I was miles away."

As they left the restaurant, Laura noted the thoughtful expression on Tanner's face and wondered at it. He was quiet throughout the drive home and though Laura tried several times to start a conversation, wanting to recapture the rapport they'd enjoyed for most of the evening, his responses were brief and hardly encouraging.

She longed to ask if she'd said or done something to cause the change in his mood, but each time she tried to broach the subject, the words froze on her lips.

Tanner brought the car to a halt outside the lodge, and before Laura could unfasten her seat belt, he was out of the car and opening the passenger door for her.

"Thank you," she said as she climbed out. "And thank you, too, for a lovely evening, Tanner."

"Are you too tired to take a walk down to the lake with me?" he asked.

"No..." She was surprised by his invitation but thought that she would gladly walk to the ends of the earth with him.

She fell into step beside him and in a matter of minutes they were standing at the lakeshore. They stood gazing out over the lake, its water as smooth as a sheet of darkly tinted glass. A silvery half moon hung lazily in the night sky, its twin sister floating on the surface of the lake. From somewhere across the water came the achingly poignant call of a loon.

"Laura." The way he spoke her name sent a shiver dancing across her skin and her heart skipped a beat as she turned to meet his gaze.

"Yes?" She found it increasingly difficult to breathe. He was much too close, his body almost touching hers, and the torment of being so achingly near and yet so far, was more than she could bear.

"I made a rather startling discovery tonight," he said in a voice that was strangely captivating.

"You did?" she responded, not exactly sure where this conversation was leading.

"I'll tell you about it in a minute," he said softly. "But there's something I need to take care of first."

"Oh... what?" she asked innocently.

"This," he said seconds before his mouth came down on hers.

The kiss was as tender and loving as anything she could have wished for. Laura swayed toward him, drawn by a magic as old as time and as powerful as the pull of gravity.

Need erupted somewhere deep in her belly, growing stronger with every heartbeat and more potent than any narcotic. His tongue paid homage to her lips before delving beyond to capture hers in a blatant dance of desire.

She was lost, lost to the power and the magic of his mouth, drinking in the nectar she'd been deprived of for too long. But even as he robbed her of the strength to resist, he was giving her everything she craved and more.

This was the reason she'd returned to Moonbeam Lake. Her heart had refused to relinquish the dream that one day she'd be reunited with her soul mate, the only man she had ever loved. Her innermost longings had been heard and answered and she could no more deny herself this glorious moment than she could reach up and steal the moon out of the sky.

He'd found nirvana and he never wanted to leave. This was where he belonged, where he always wanted to be; here with this woman.

He'd experienced this earth-shattering emotion only once before in his life, and as the blood began to hum through his veins he was almost sure that the woman in his arms felt as strongly and as passionately as he did.

He'd read, with a mixture of fascination and skepticism, about men and women in search of their soul mates. But not until this moment did he truly understand what that meant.

Laura was his soul mate, his one true love. She was as much a part of him as he was of her. Six years ago they'd come together during a time of darkness and emotional chaos. But fate had conspired against them— sending them off in opposite directions.

But some deep inner instinct had recognized then the love they'd been destined to share, and fate had stepped in once more to bring them both back to the same place, at the same time, for the sole purpose of rediscovering each other.

Slowly, reluctantly, Tanner broke the kiss and not without some effort pulled back from the brink. His senses were overloading, his body throbbing with a need that threatened to overwhelm him, but it wasn't enough... he wanted more... he wanted it all.

"Laura?" His voice vibrated with tension as he grimly held on to his self-control. "Why did you agree to marry me?"

Tanner's question barely registered as Laura fought to regain her shattered composure. Feeling more than a little dizzy from the flight to heaven and back, her body was silently screaming in protest at being deprived of the sustenance it had craved for so long.

Tanner's kiss had effectively torn down the wall she'd erected around her emotions, leaving her open and vulnerable.

"What?" she mumbled breathlessly.

"Why did you agree to marry me?" he repeated.

Laura met Tanner's gaze and her body stilled at the look she could see in his eyes, an unfathomable look. "Ah...the twins, they need a father...they need *their* father," she corrected, desperately trying to say the words he wanted to hear.

"And what about you, Laura? What do you need?" he asked, an urgency in his voice she found disconcerting.

"Me?" said Laura bewildered by the question. "I don't understand..."

Fear suddenly clutched at Tanner's insides. He'd been so sure the reason she'd agreed to marry him was that her feelings for him were as strong and deep as his feelings for her. Was he wrong?

No! He couldn't be wrong. Stubbornly he clung to the memory of the way she'd responded to his kiss a moment ago. He was right. He had to be. Their future depended on it. And suddenly he knew that it was all up to him, that he had to bare his heart and soul and trust in his instincts.

He drew a steadying breath and threw caution to the wind. "I was hoping you would say that I'm the one you need," he said softly, "because tonight I realized that as much as I love the twins, they're not the only reason I wanted us to get married."

Laura's heart leaped into her throat as she met his gaze and saw fear and vulnerability lurking in the depths of his eyes.

"What other reason is there?" she asked breathlessly, half-afraid to hope, yet brave enough to want to know the answer.

"You're not going to make this easy, are you?" she heard Tanner say almost to himself.

Laura gasped in astonishment when Tanner suddenly dropped to one knee on the rocks in front of her.

Taking her hand in his, he gazed up at her. "I didn't just ask you to marry me because of the twins. I asked you to marry me because I love you—truly, madly, deeply. I want you to be my wife, my partner, my lover, my friend. Laura, will you marry me?"

Laura stood staring down at Tanner, wondering if this was all a dream. Tears stung her eyes and there was a lump in her throat that refused to budge.

This couldn't be happening! Had Tanner really said those wonderful, beautiful, incredibly romantic things? She closed her eyes for a fleeting second, sure that when she opened them again he would have vanished.

From somewhere out on the water the mournful cry of a loon suddenly echoed through the still night air, touching a chord deep inside her.

"Laura?"

The way he spoke her name was like a plea and at the sound of his voice Laura opened her eyes to see Tanner gazing up at her with a look that sent a delicious thrill chasing through her.

She swallowed convulsively and managed to find her voice. "I said yes before and I'll say it again, because I want to be your wife, your partner, your lover and your friend," she said softly and sincerely.

Stunned for a moment, Tanner just stared at her. Then, with a mixture of relief and excitement, he kissed the back of her hand before turning it over and pressing his lips to the delicate skin at her wrist and trailing a path to the center of her hand.

He felt the quiver of need beneath his lips and reveled in her response. He stood up but controlled the urge to haul her into his arms.

"I'm afraid that's not quite enough," he said, his voice husky with emotion. "I need to know you feel the same. I need to hear you say it." He held her gaze with an intensity that was shattering.

With courage and love Tanner had handed her his heart and it was only fair that she give him hers in return.

"Six years ago, on a night I will never forget, I became a woman in the truest sense of the word. I think I loved you then almost as much as I love you now," she told him with an honesty that took his breath away.

With a moan of triumph, Tanner swooped down and covered her mouth with his.

They clung to each other for what seemed an eternity and when at last they came up for air, Tanner was the first to speak.

"If this is a dream, don't ever wake me," he said in a voice roughened with desire.

Laura laughed as she brushed her lips against his jaw. "We must be having the same dream," she said, her heart bursting with love.

Tanner's low rumble of laughter joined hers and he kissed her hard on the mouth, then pulled away. "There's so much I want to say, to ask," he went on.

"And now we have a lifetime..." Laura said.

"We do indeed," Tanner said before he claimed her lips once more.

Epilogue

Laura stood at the kitchen window taking in the magnificent view of Vancouver's skyline. She was waiting for Tanner. He'd just called to say he was on his way home and that he had exciting news.

She'd refrained from mentioning that she had some news of her own, and she smiled to herself for a moment wondering just what his reaction would be when she told him she was pregnant.

There were times Laura still found it hard to believe that the man she'd loved for so long was her husband and had been for the past three hundred and sixty-five glorious days.

She had never loved Tanner more, or been more proud of him than when he'd suggested that they start off their new life together by telling the children and Mac the truth about the past. The news had been received with whoops of joy from the children and tears of happiness from their grandfather.

During the past year her life and the twins' had undergone a number of changes. Shortly after the wedding, they'd all moved to this beautiful five bedroom house on the city's north shore. The children were attending a school nearby and because they adored their father, they'd quickly adjusted to having him around on a permanent basis.

Today the house was quiet. The twins were spending the weekend with Mac at Moonbeam Lake. Irene had come to collect them that morning and would be bringing them back with her on Monday.

Laura heard Tanner's car pull into the driveway and a ripple of excitement and anticipation swept through her as she waited for him to join her.

He'd told her that morning he'd made a reservation for dinner at their favorite restaurant to celebrate their anniversary and she was looking forward to the evening ahead.

"Laura?"

"In here!" she responded as she turned to greet him.

"Happy anniversary, darling," Tanner said as he appeared in the doorway.

Laura's mouth dropped open in astonishment when she saw the enormous bouquet of red roses Tanner was holding in his arms.

"Oh...Tanner, they're beautiful." She crossed to him and taking the flowers from him, smiled and kissed him lightly, teasingly on his lips. "Thank you," she said enjoying the intoxicating scent floating around her.

Tanner leaned over to capture her mouth once more in a kiss that instantly set her on fire.

"That's just an appetizer," he told her as he pulled away. "First things first. I want to tell you my news."

"What did the publisher say?" Laura asked, having difficulty controlling the urge to kiss him again. She turned and put the flowers on the counter.

"That he thinks my photographs are fabulous and he likes the idea of a nature book suitable for young children," Tanner said.

Laura threw him a startled glance. "You mean he's given you the go ahead?"

"I mean, I just signed a contract," came the reply.

"Tanner, that's wonderful! Congratulations!"

"Thank you." He grinned at her. "Oh...there is one more thing," he went on. "I was going to wait until dinner to give you this, but it's been burning a hole in my pocket all day."

From his jacket pocket he withdrew a small velvet covered box and opening the lid, held it out to her.

Laura almost fainted at the sight of the ring nestled in the silky red folds of the box. Diamonds and sapphires arranged in a delicate gold setting dazzled her and Laura's throat closed over with emotion.

"Oh...Tanner." Her voice wobbled and the tears gathering in her eyes spilled over.

"Darling...don't cry." Tanner's voice was achingly tender.

"I can't help it," Laura said with a sob. "This is so romantic..." she broke off, unable to continue.

Taking her left hand in his, Tanner slid the ring onto her fourth finger, until it came to rest next to the wide gold wedding band he'd put there exactly a year ago.

Laura smiled at him through her tears. "I have a present for you, too, but I can't give it to you yet," she said softly.

"Why not? What is it?"

She drew a steadying breath. "Actually, you'll have to wait another eight months for delivery," she told him, love and laughter echoing in her voice.

"Eight months?" Tanner repeated in a puzzled tone.

Laura nodded and moved into the warm haven of his arms, watching as the impact of her words hit home.

"You don't mean...are we? Are you?" Tanner could scarcely formulate the question.

"Yes. Yes. And yes," she replied, happiness rippling through her.

Tanner's mouth swooped down on hers sending them both into a mindless orbit. Several minutes passed before they returned once more to earth.

"You've given me so much already," Tanner said in a throaty whisper. "Do you know how much I love you?" he asked as he lifted her into his arms and carried her into the hallway.

Laura sighed and nuzzled his neck. "I thought you were taking me out for supper...to celebrate our anniversary."

Tanner laughed, a rich sound that sent shivers chasing through her. "Oh...we'll celebrate all right. Make no mistake about that..."

Cradling her against his chest, he began to climb the stairs to their bedroom.

* * * * *

**HE'S MORE THAN
A MAN, HE'S
ONE OF OUR**

EMMETT
Diana Palmer

What a way to start the new year! Not only is Diana Palmer's
EMMETT the first of our new series, FABULOUS FATHERS, but
it's her 10th LONG, TALL TEXANS and her 50th book for
Silhouette!

Emmett Deverell was at the end of his lasso. His three children
had become uncontrollable! The long, tall Texan knew they
needed a mother's influence, and the only female offering was
Melody Cartman. Emmett would rather be tied to a cactus than
deal with that prickly woman. But Melody proved to be softer
than he'd ever imagined....

Don't miss Diana Palmer's EMMETT, available in January.

Fall in love with our FABULOUS FATHERS—and join the
Silhouette Romance family!

Silhouette
R O M A N C E™

FF193

Silhouette
R O M A N C E™

HEARTLAND HOLIDAYS

Christmas bells turn into wedding bells for the Gallagher siblings in Stella Bagwell's *Heartland Holidays* trilogy.

THEIR FIRST THANKSGIVING (#903) in November
Olivia Westcott had once rejected Sam Gallagher's proposal—and in his stubborn pride, he'd refused to hear her reasons why. Now Olivia is back...and it is about time Sam Gallagher listened!

THE BEST CHRISTMAS EVER (#909) in December
Soldier Nick Gallagher had come home to be the best man at his brother's wedding—not to be a groom! But when he met single mother Allison Lee, he knew he'd found his bride.

NEW YEAR'S BABY (#915) in January
Kathleen Gallagher had given up on love and marriage until she came to the rescue of neighbor Ross Douglas . . . and the newborn baby he'd found on his doorstep!

Come celebrate the holidays with Silhouette Romance!

NORA ROBERTS

Love has a language all its own, and for centuries
flowers have symbolized love's finest expression.
Discover the language of flowers—and love—in
this romantic collection of 48 favorite books by
bestselling author Nora Roberts.

Two titles are available each month at your
favorite retail outlet.

In December, look for:

Partners, **Volume #21**
Sullivan's Woman, **Volume #22**

In January, look for:

Summer Desserts, **Volume #23**
This Magic Moment, **Volume #24**

Collect all 48 titles
and become fluent in **THE LANGUAGE of LOVE**

VOWS
A series celebrating marriage
by Sherryl Woods

To Love, Honor and Cherish—these were the words that three generations of Halloran men promised their women they'd live by. But these vows made in love are each challenged by the tests of time....

In October—Jason Halloran meets his match in *Love* #769;
In November—Kevin Halloran rediscovers love—with his wife—in *Honor* #775;
In December—Brandon Halloran rekindles an old flame in *Cherish* #781.

These three stirring tales are coming down the aisle toward you—only from Silhouette Special Edition!

Silhouette Christmas Stories 1992

Experience the beauty of Yuletide romance with Silhouette Christmas Stories 1992—a collection of heartwarming stories by favorite Silhouette authors.

JONI'S MAGIC by Mary Lynn Baxter
HEARTS OF HOPE by Sondra Stanford
THE NIGHT SANTA CLAUS RETURNED by Marie Ferrarella
BASKET OF LOVE by Jeanne Stephens

Also available this year are three popular early editions of Silhouette Christmas Stories—1986, 1987 and 1988. Look for these and you'll be well on your way to a complete collection of the best in holiday romance.

Plus, as an added bonus, you can receive a FREE keepsake Christmas ornament. Just collect four proofs of purchase from any November or December 1992 Harlequin or Silhouette series novels, or from any Harlequin or Silhouette Christmas collection, and receive a beautiful dated brass Christmas candle ornament.

Mail this certificate along with four (4) proof-of-purchase coupons, plus $1.50 postage and handling (check or money order—do not send cash), payable to Silhouette Books, to: **In the U.S.:** P.O. Box 9057, Buffalo, NY 14269-9057; **In Canada:** P.O. Box 622, Fort Erie, Ontario, L2A 5X3.

ONE PROOF OF PURCHASE	Name: _____
SX92POP	Address: _____
	City: _____
	State/Province: _____
	Zip/Postal Code: _____

093 KAG